Elizabeth had seen enough police shows to know what a holding cell looked like, but seeing one on television and actually being locked inside one were two very different things. She almost screamed out loud when the door banged shut behind her. *Don't leave me here by myself!* she wanted to beg. *Please, please don't leave me by myself.* But she didn't. She faced the cell with the same resolve that had helped her through her arrest and interrogation. Feeling as though she were crossing an enormous desert, she slowly walked the few feet between the door and the wall and sat down in the farthest corner. She was able to shed her facade of assurance, and she wanted to disappear.

It took a few seconds for Elizabeth to realize that she wasn't alone in the cell. Two other women shared the small space. The first was a heavily made-up, disheveled, middle-aged woman. The second was a girl not much older than Elizabeth.

Though she tried to ignore them, Elizabeth could feel them staring at her with hostility.

The woman suddenly launched herself off the hard wooden bench.

"Whatsa matta, honey?" she demanded, staggering toward Elizabeth. "You get caught driving your daddy's Porsche too fast?"

Elizabeth desperately wished that she were invisible.

SWEET VALLEY High®

THE ARREST

Written by
Kate William

Created by
FRANCINE PASCAL

BANTAM BOOKS
NEW YORK • TORONTO • LONDON • SYDNEY • AUCKLAND

RL 6, age 12 and up

THE ARREST

A Bantam Book / August 1993

Sweet Valley High® is a registered trademark of Francine Pascal
Conceived by Francine Pascal
Produced by Daniel Weiss Associates, Inc.
33 West 17th Street
New York, NY 10011
Cover art by Joe Danisi

ISBN: 0-553-29853-4

Published simultaneously in the United States and Canada

Bantam Books are published by Bantam Books, a division of Bantam
Doubleday Dell Publishing Group, Inc. Its trademark, consisting of the
words "Bantam Books" and the portrayal of a rooster, is Registered in
U.S. Patent and Trademark Office and in other countries. Marca
Registrada. Bantam Books, 1540 Broadway, New York, New York 10036.

PRINTED IN THE UNITED STATES OF AMERICA

OPM   0 9 8 7 6 5

Chapter 1

Elizabeth Wakefield sat at a large wooden table, her damp hands clasped in front of her. Her heart was pounding, and her usually sparkling blue-green eyes were filled with confusion and pain. *This can't really be happening,* she thought desperately. *It just can't be.* She bit her lip so hard that she was sure it would begin to bleed. *It must be a dream,* she told herself. *That's it. A bad, bad dream. A nightmare. I'll wake up soon and I'll be safe at home in my own bed, and the sun will be shining through the window and my mother will be yelling at us to get up.*

Slowly, almost painfully, Elizabeth raised her eyes from the table and looked around her. She was in a bare, beige room whose small, dirty windows were set high in the walls and covered with steel grating. The room was illuminated by a single fluorescent light overhead. Her father, Ned Wakefield, sat beside her, one arm around her thin shoulders while he drummed restlessly on the table with his other hand. Across from her, serious and unsmiling, Detectives Marsh and Perez silently read through the typewritten pages before them.

An unbearable coldness settled in Elizabeth's stomach. This wasn't a nightmare. This was really happening. She wasn't going to wake up back on Calico Drive to the comforting aroma of freshly brewed coffee and the busy sound of the morning radio show. She wasn't going to hear her mother calling her for breakfast or her twin sister, Jessica, noisily getting ready for school in the room next to hers. At the thought of Jessica, hot tears stung Elizabeth's eyes. She wiped them away with the tissue balled up in her fist.

No, this wasn't a dream. This was reality. Her reality. She really was sitting in an interrogation room at the Sweet Valley Police Station. She really was being questioned by Detective Roger Marsh and Detective Andrew Perez about the fatal car crash that had killed her sister's boyfriend, Sam Woodruff, a few nights ago.

Fresh, sharp tears spilled down her cheeks. All at once Elizabeth was transported back to that awful night, the night of the Jungle Prom.

The barren room, the unsmiling policemen, and even her worried father vanished. All she could see was the black road and a sudden, frantic swirl of headlights; all she could hear was the terrified screech of brakes and the angry sound of shattering glass.

"Miss Wakefield? Elizabeth?"

Her father squeezed her shoulder. "Detective Marsh was asking you a question," he whispered.

Elizabeth blinked. Detective Marsh was leaning toward her, a concerned expression on his face. "Miss Wakefield," he repeated. "Miss Wakefield, are you all right?"

All right? Elizabeth wondered silently. *What is all right supposed to mean when you're overcome with so much misery and sorrow?* But she nodded automatically. Calling on all her will, she managed to whisper, "Yes." Her father's hand tightened on her arm. "Yes, I'm all—all right."

"We have to ask you just a few more questions," said Detective Marsh. "It won't take long."

Ned Wakefield drew himself up straight. "I really don't see why this is necessary," he said in his most authoritative manner. "This has been a terrible ordeal for Elizabeth. You can see for yourselves that she's still in shock."

Detective Perez moved his chair back from the table. The scraping sound ran down Elizabeth's spine like a knife.

"We appreciate what your daughter has gone through, Mr. Wakefield," he said in a flat, impersonal voice. "But you're a lawyer yourself. This may not be your usual sort of case, but I'm sure you understand that we're only doing our job. We have to examine all the evidence. There are things that have come up. . . ." Detective Perez lowered his voice. "A boy is dead, Mr. Wakefield. We take that very seriously."

At the mention of Sam, his face flashed in front of Elizabeth's eyes. He was smiling in his warm, easy way. He looked so real, just for that instant, that she almost felt as though she could reach out and touch him. She had to hold her breath to stop herself from crying again. *All right?* she thought hopelessly. *I may never be all right again.*

Her father was still holding on to her. He nodded at Detective Perez. "I do understand," he said evenly. "Of course I understand. It was a terrible thing that happened. But I want my daughter to understand that as long as no charges have been filed against her, she is under no legal obligation to answer your questions."

The two detectives looked at each other.

"Dad—" Elizabeth had been listening to her

father and the policeman talking as though they were in another room, talking about somebody else, but now she reached out and put her hand over Mr. Wakefield's. "It's OK, Dad," she said in a hushed, strained voice. "I'll answer whatever I can."

Detective Marsh smiled at her. "Thank you, Miss Wakefield. You're very brave." He glanced at the paper in front of him again. "Now, according to your original statement, you don't remember leaving the dance."

Elizabeth closed her eyes, trying to put aside the moment of the crash itself and get back to the Jungle Prom. But there wasn't anything before the crash; nothing at all. She opened her eyes again and made herself look at Detective Marsh. "No," she said, shaking her head. "No, I don't remember."

Detective Perez tipped his chair back. "You must remember something, Miss Wakefield," he pressed. "What about *why* you left the dance? Was it because your twin sister, Jessica Wakefield, and your boyfriend, Todd Wilkins, were voted Prom Queen and King? Could that have been the reason?"

"Now see here!" Ned Wakefield slammed his fist on the table so hard that Elizabeth jumped. "I don't think you have any right—"

Detective Marsh's calm, even voice cut him

off. "There's no need to get upset, Mr. Wake-field," he said reassuringly. "All Detective Perez is trying to do is help jog Elizabeth's memory. We were hoping she might have some idea of where she and Mr. Woodruff were going when they left the school." He turned to his partner. "Isn't that right, Andrew?"

Elizabeth focused her eyes on the tabletop again, but she could still feel the others looking at her. The policemen were eyeing her with suspicion; her father with concern. In her mind, brakes were screeching and glass was splintering around her like a shower of stars. Oh, how she wished she *could* remember something. How she wished she could go back to that night and live it all over again.

"I truly don't remember," she finally choked out. "I guess we were driving along and then there was all this noise . . . this horrible noise. . . . I must have hit the brakes, and the windshield started to break. . . ." She wondered if the others could hear the pounding of her heart. "I'm really, really sorry," she whispered, "but I don't remember anything more than that. I just don't."

Elizabeth steeled herself against another attack of tears. During this horrible nightmare, the fact that she couldn't remember what had happened that night was in some ways the worst thing of all. She remembered the days leading up to the gala Jungle Prom. She remembered the fierce competition between herself and Jessica to see who would be selected Queen. She even remembered that she'd been trying to be a new person—a more assertive and less giving person, a person more like her flamboyant twin. But when she tried to think of the dance itself, her mind went blank. No, not even blank. There was a hole in her mind where her memories of the dance should have been. Memories of what she did, whom she talked to, why she and Sam left together, and where they were going. . . . It was as though several hours of her life had been ripped out like pages from a book. Ripped out and thrown away.

Detective Perez cleared his throat. "I'm afraid that the lab report showed a significant blood-alcohol level in both your daughter and Sam Woodruff." He tapped the report on the table. "I'm sorry, Mr. Wakefield, but on the basis of that and the other evidence we have, added to Elizabeth's complete inability to offer anything in her defense . . ." Detective Perez paused and shook his head sadly. "Well, I'm afraid that we're going to have to charge her with involuntary manslaughter."

Elizabeth could feel what was left of her control slipping away. The room began to spin around her; her head started to throb. She bit her lip to try to keep the tears back, to try to keep herself from trembling with sobs. Manslaughter! They were accusing her of killing Sam. She was going to jail!

"Don't worry, honey," her father was saying from somewhere about a million miles away. "This is all a mistake. A dreadful mistake. Don't you worry, I'm going to get you the best defense lawyer money can buy. We'll have them apologizing publicly before we're through."

But Elizabeth couldn't concentrate on what her father was telling her. All she could think of was Sam. Sam was dead and it hadn't been an unavoidable accident. Sam was dead and it was she who had murdered him.

Elizabeth had seen enough police shows to know what a holding cell looked like, but seeing one on television and actually being locked inside one were two very different things. She almost screamed out loud when the door banged shut behind her. *Don't leave me here by myself!* she wanted to beg. *Please, please don't leave me by myself.* But she didn't. She faced the cell with the same resolve that had helped her through her arrest and interrogation. Feeling as though she were crossing an enormous desert, she slowly walked the few feet between the door and the wall and sat down in the farthest corner.

8

She was able to shed her facade of assurance, and she wanted to disappear.

It took a few seconds for Elizabeth to realize that she wasn't alone in the cell. Two other women shared the small space. The first was a heavily made-up, disheveled, middle-aged woman who was slumped against the opposite wall, breathing loudly. The second was a girl not much older than Elizabeth. She was also wearing a lot of makeup, and was dressed in a short, tight, satin skirt, a skimpy silver halter top, and glittering silvery stockings.

Though she tried to ignore them, Elizabeth could feel them staring at her with hostility.

The woman suddenly launched herself off the hard wooden bench.

"Whatsa matta, honey?" she demanded, staggering toward Elizabeth. "You get caught driving your daddy's Porsche too fast?"

Elizabeth desperately wished that she were invisible.

The girl's eyes looked up and down Elizabeth as though she were a dress she was thinking of buying.

"You know what?" the girl asked in a slow, wry drawl. "Lucky for me she's not in my line of work." She laughed. "She could make a fortune with that California beach-girl look of hers. That drives the guys nuts."

Elizabeth huddled into her corner, hoping the others couldn't see how she was blushing. *Don't listen,* she told herself, refusing to look at her cellmates. *Don't listen. And don't speak.* If she ignored them, maybe they'd leave her alone.

"Come on, princess," the woman taunted her. "Tell us what you're in here for." She lurched closer, coming to an unsteady stop at Elizabeth's side. She was so close that Elizabeth could smell the alcohol on her breath. "Bet you've never been in a place like this before, have ya, honey? Bet you can't wait to get back to your nice family and all your nice rich friends."

"How can you say a thing like that?" the girl asked, almost offended. "I'm sure the princess finds her fancy suburban life totally boring. I'm sure she'd much rather be here with us." She slapped the cinder-block stone wall. "It's so much cozier in a jail cell than it is in a big expensive house."

Elizabeth dug her nails into the palms of her hands, willing herself not to collapse completely. *Please,* she silently pleaded. *Please just let me get through this. Don't let me start crying now.*

Elizabeth understood that ever since the night of the crash, part of her had been numb. Most of her was torn apart with guilt and grief, but there had been a small part that had felt nothing. That small section of her heart and mind was what had gotten her through Sam's funeral and allowed her to get from one bleak day to the next. It had allowed her to go on, even though Jessica and Todd Wilkins, the two people she loved most in the world, had barely spoken a word to her since the night of the crash. But now, sitting in the cold, dingy cell, staring at the shadows of the iron bars on the floor, the numbness was beginning to seep away.

It was leaving, but it was being replaced by terror. Elizabeth had never felt so alone or so frightened before in her life.

Against her will, her body began to shake with silent sobs.

"Whatsa matter, honey?" the woman jeered at her again. "You want your daddy to come and take you home? You missin' your favorite TV show or couldn't you get a date on a Saturday night?"

The girl threw herself on the bench. "Oh, leave her alone, why don't you?" she snapped. Her voice was loud and tough. "Can't you see the poor kid's upset? Why don't you do us all a favor and just sit down and pass out?"

Hugging herself as tightly as she could, Elizabeth looked gratefully up at the girl through her tears.

"You just go on and let it all out," the girl advised her. "It'll make you feel better. Really. It will."

But Elizabeth knew that she might never feel better again.

Amy Sutton watched warily as Lila Fowler dragged more and more clothes out of her enormous closet and spread them on the bed for Amy's approval.

Lila was not only one of the prettiest and most popular girls in Sweet Valley, she was also one of the wealthiest. Which meant that if she was going to make Amy look at everything in her wardrobe, they might be here for the rest of the week, or at least the rest of the weekend.

Lila picked up a soft cotton dress in a delicate shade of lilac and held it away from her. "You know, I've always been partial to purple," she said, eyeing it critically. "But I'm sure I once heard my father say that my mother couldn't stand purple, unless it was on a plum!" She laughed as though this were the funniest thing she had ever heard.

Amy smiled woodenly. The size of Lila's wardrobe wasn't the only reason Amy was nervous. An amazing change had come over Lila in just a few days. Lila had been going through a bad time recently. It had started with John Pfeiffer and blown up with Nathan Pritchard, and she'd become unusually silent and withdrawn. She'd stopped dating. She'd stopped hanging out with her friends. She'd even stopped shopping and gossiping, her two favorite activities. Today, however, she seemed as happy as a cheerleader at the Rose Bowl—and more like her old self than her old self had been.

Lila wiped tears of laughter from her eyes. "Gosh," she said. "I can't seem to stop talking today. I guess I'm just nervous about seeing Grace after all these years."

Grace, Amy repeated silently. She was already tired of hearing the name. Ever since she'd arrived, everything had been Grace this and Grace that. *Maybe Grace would like this. Maybe Grace wouldn't like that. Maybe Grace and I will go away for a weekend. Maybe Grace and I will go to the theater. I wonder what Grace's favorite food is?*

Amy forced another smile on her lips. "Well, it isn't every day you meet your long-lost mother, is it?" she asked brightly. "I mean, it's been a long time since your parents were divorced. You're bound to be a little edgy."

"That's true, isn't it?" asked Lila. "I mean, I *should* be nervous. In six days I'm finally going to meet my mother for the first time since I was two! But then again, she *is* my mother." Lila laughed again.

Amy sighed inwardly. Sometimes she couldn't help thinking that Lila was the classic poor little rich girl. Lila might have everything money could buy, but there were things that money *couldn't* buy that she needed desperately. Things like her busy father's time and companionship, and her mother's presence and love.

Lila's laughter bounced through the room again. "I just want to look perfect, that's all. After all, Grace does live in Paris. I don't want her to think I'm too provincial." Frowning, she picked a pair of black silk pants off the pile. "On the other hand," she continued, "I don't want her to think I'm *too* sophisticated. I mean, the last time she saw me I was a little kid. I want her to remember me like that, too. You know, so we can bond."

Amy was grateful that Lila's attention was back on her clothes so that Lila couldn't see the expression on Amy's face. *So they could bond?* It was all Amy could do to keep from laughing out loud. The only times she'd ever heard Lila Fowler use the word "bond" was when the word "stock" was right before it.

"I'm sure she remembers you from when you were little," Amy said reassuringly. But to herself she added, *How else is she going to remember Lila? She's never even seen her with a full set of teeth.*

Amy sighed again as she finally realized what

was bothering her. There was something too unreal about this whole reunion between Lila and her mother. It was as though Lila thought that being reunited with Grace Fowler was going to solve every problem she'd ever had, once and for all.

"It's just that I want to make a good impression," Lila was saying. "I don't want to wear the wrong thing."

"She's your mother, Lila," Amy said gently but firmly. "You wouldn't be wearing the wrong thing if you showed up in a shopping bag."

Lila emerged from the closet with yet another armload of clothes. "Do you really think so?" she asked eagerly.

"Of course I do," Amy said. "I'll bet she's as nervous about meeting you as you are about meeting her."

"Really?" Lila dumped the clothes on the bed.

"Of course really," Amy said. "I'll bet right this minute she's going through *her* closet, trying to decide what to wear."

Lila picked up a cream-colored linen suit and held it against her. "I wish I didn't have to wait so long to see her!" She laughed. "I don't know how I'm going to get through the next six days."

"You've gotten through the last fourteen

years," mumbled Amy, "this should be nothing." But Lila wasn't listening.

"I bet Grace will have a special present for me, you know, to mark the occasion," she said. Frown lines appeared on her forehead. "Do you think I should get something for her, Amy?" She dropped the suit on top of the silk pants. "But what? I don't know what she likes. Or what she has. She probably already has everything." The frown lines grew deeper. "I guess I could get her some flowers, a big bunch of roses or orchids or something. But what if she's allergic? Or if she doesn't like flowers? What if—"

Amy had to cut her off before she screamed. "Lila, listen to me," she said softly. She got up and went to stand next to her friend, pretending to be going through the clothes. She cleared her throat. "I do think maybe you shouldn't get yourself so wound up about this. Try to relax a little. I mean, it has been years . . . it'll take a long time for you and your mother to really get to know each other—"

"But she's my mother," protested Lila. "It's not like meeting a perfect stranger, is it? As soon as we see each other, everything will fall into place." She fingered the hem of a white silk dress. "Then everything will be all right," she added in almost a whisper. "Everything will be fine again."

"Lila . . ." Amy reached out and put a hand on Lila's shoulder. "Lila, I really think you should be a little . . . a little careful. You don't want to get hurt. You want—"

Lila turned around so suddenly she nearly knocked Amy off balance. "What are you saying?" She was staring at her with an expression that was half angry, half puzzled. "Are you saying that you think Grace won't like me? Is that what you're saying? That you think she'll be disappointed in me?"

Amy's heart thudded. One of the things Amy was most afraid of was that the wonderful Grace might take one look at Lila and wish she'd stayed in France. The other was that Lila might take one look at the wonderful Grace and wish she'd never come back into her life.

"Of course not," said Amy quickly. "All I meant was—"

"That *is* what you meant!" Lila cried accusingly. "You're trying to ruin the best thing that's happened to me in years."

"Lila, that's ridiculous," Amy defended herself. "You know I'm not trying to ruin anything. I'm trying to help."

"Help? This is your idea of helping? Undermining my confidence?"

Amy wished that Jessica Wakefield were here now. Jessica and Lila were not only best friends, but Jessica knew how to make Lila listen to reason. But Jessica had some very serious problems of her own at the moment. No one, not even Lila, had seen very much of Jessica since Sam's funeral. You couldn't expect Jessica to be concerned about Lila's mother when she was getting over her boyfriend's death, the boyfriend her twin sister had killed.

"I thought you'd be a little more sympathetic," Lila snapped. "After all, this is an incredible opportunity for me."

The ringing of Lila's blue princess phone saved Amy from having to get deeper into what she could already see was a useless argument.

Lila lifted the receiver. "Hello," she said coolly.

Almost instantly the expression on her face changed to one of pure rapture.

"Mothe—Grace!"

Amy bit her lip, her whole body tense with anxiety. What if Lila and Grace didn't even meet before they started disappointing each other? But within a few seconds she began to relax. It was clear from the way Lila was smiling and nodding that her mother was saying all the right things. Every so often there'd be a few seconds of silence, and then Lila would say enthusiastically, "Oh, me too. I'm really

18

looking forward to it too. I can't wait. I'll see you then."

At last she put the receiver back in its cradle. "That was my mother . . . Grace . . . that was her," she announced. When Lila turned around, her eyes were filled with tears.

"She just wanted me to know that she can't wait to see me again," Lila whispered. "Isn't that great? She said she can't stop thinking about me, and she just wanted me to know that."

Impulsively, Amy put her arms around Lila's shaking shoulders. *Please God,* she prayed silently. *Please let this be all right.*

Steven Wakefield paced restlessly through the rooms of his new off-campus apartment. When he'd first seen it, he'd thought it was enormous, with its two bedrooms, living room, and eat-in kitchen. But today it seemed as small as a prison cell. As small as the cell where his sister was sitting at this very moment, lonely and afraid.

Ever since Ned Wakefield phoned him to tell him that the police had filed charges against Elizabeth, Steven had been unable to think of anything but her. All morning he had been waiting for his father to call back with news. His instincts had told him that it didn't look good for his sister.

Steven glanced over at the telephone, willing it to ring. Why wasn't his father calling? What was taking so long?

"It isn't fair!" Steven said out loud. "It just isn't fair."

Desperate to take his mind off Elizabeth for even a few minutes, Steven picked up the college newspaper from the table beside the phone. He flicked to the back. The new semester had just started, so there were all the usual ads for used books and bands needing guitarists. What Steven needed, however, was not a bass player or a secondhand sociology text. What he needed was a roommate. Not that he held out much hope of finding one. Since it was the middle of the year, most people already had their accommodations. And then a small ad at the bottom of the page caught his eye: "Mature and considerate student looking for immediate apartment share. 555-1232. Ask for Billie Winkler."

Steven took a pen out of his pocket and circled the number. *Mature . . . considerate . . . immediate . . .* "Sounds too good to be true," he told himself, but his hand reached out to dial the number.

Before he could lift the receiver, however, the phone began to ring. Steven was so sure it must be his father that he didn't even bother to say hello.

"What happened?" he demanded. "How's Liz?"

Ned Wakefield coughed. Steven had heard him cough in exactly that way thousands of times in the past, usually when he had some bad news to give to a client.

"Dad?" Steven had to use all his control not to shout. "Dad, what's happened?"

"I'm afraid we've had a temporary setback," Mr. Wakefield said slowly but calmly.

"Setback?" Steven could hear the shrillness in his own voice. "What kind of setback?"

Ned Wakefield coughed again. "Elizabeth is still in custody at the police station. They're making her spend the night."

The newspaper slipped off Steven's lap. The room began to rock back and forth.

"Steven?" There was the slightest edge of panic in Ned Wakefield's voice. "Steven, are you still there?"

"Not for much longer," said Steven, jumping to his feet. "I'm coming home. My place is in Sweet Valley with you guys."

"Don't be ridiculous." His father's tone was firm. "You've just started a new term. There's nothing you can do here now, and in any event the situation is under control."

Once more, Steven had to stop himself from shouting. "I don't see how you can say the situation is under control when Elizabeth is in jail," he said evenly. "That doesn't sound like control to me."

"Steven, please." His father sighed, betraying the strain and weariness he was feeling. "There really is nothing you can do here. Elizabeth will be out any time now, and I've retained the best defense lawyer in California for the job."

"But I—"

"I know, Steven. You want Liz to know that you're with her on this. She knows that. Just as we know she's innocent. Whatever happened that night was not her fault; I'm as sure of that as I am of my own name. Once this fiasco comes to trial we'll prove that, and then this whole thing will seem like nothing more than a bad dream."

"I hope you're right about that," Steven said flatly. He could see the sense of what his father was saying. Probably the last thing his parents needed was to have to worry about him missing school on top of everything else. But that didn't change the fact that he felt he should be by Elizabeth's side.

"I *am* right," said Ned Wakefield, his voice filling with his usual confidence. "Trust me on this, Steven. It won't be long before this nightmare is over, believe me."

But as he hung up the phone, Steven found

himself thinking, *What if you're wrong, Dad? What if this nightmare has just begun?*

All Sunday while they pretended to go about their lives as usual, the Wakefields had their minds on Elizabeth. Was she all right? How could they help her? When would this all be behind them? Even Prince Albert, the Wakefields's golden retriever, lay by the back door, his large eyes sad, his ears pricking up every time he heard something outside, waiting for Elizabeth to come back home.

Jessica wasn't thinking only about her sister. In her mind, thoughts of Elizabeth were irrevocably tangled with thoughts of Sam.

Her golden-blond hair shining in the sunlight, her blue-green eyes staring blindly into the distance, Jessica sat at her bedroom window like a princess in a tower. Only there would be no prince coming for this princess. No handsome young knight on a white charger to rescue her from her misery and make all her dreams come true. Not now.

Jessica looked down to the street below. Children were playing on lawns; kids were riding their bikes up Calico Drive. Everything was just as it had always been. Except for one thing. One small, insignificant detail that maybe thirty or forty people in the world even cared about.

Sam Woodruff was dead. That was the only difference between today and any day only a week or so ago. Sam was dead. She would never see him turn into the driveway, honking his horn in his special signal. She would never again see him striding across the lawn with Prince Albert at his heels. She would never again feel his arm around her or hear him whisper her name.

Jessica leaned her head against the windowpane. For the first day or so after the accident, she'd been in shock. She'd refused to believe that Sam wasn't still alive. "It has to be a mistake," she kept saying. "It wasn't Sam in the car, it was someone who looked like him." Jessica had been too upset to go to the funeral.

Jessica pushed the thought of the prom and what she'd done that night from her mind. She didn't like to think about how she'd spiked Elizabeth's and Sam's drinks. She wouldn't think about it. She would concentrate on coming to terms with Sam's death. She'd forget about the dance, and she'd concentrate on feeling better, on getting over Sam and starting again. That was what everyone said she should do, get over Sam and start again.

A teenage boy wearing a baseball cap just like Sam's skated past the Wakefields' house. Jessica's eyes followed him down the street.

At least she'd finally stopped crying. In fact,

she didn't think she *could* cry anymore. There were no tears left. She was empty inside. Empty and very cold. *That's what happens when you come to terms with somebody's death,* she told herself. *You feel empty and cold inside, and the tears just dry up.*

The boy on the Rollerblades even looked a little like Sam. He had the same build and coloring; he leaned the way she'd seen Sam lean when he was taking a turn on his dirt bike.

One single tear made its way down Jessica's smooth, tanned cheek. "Sam," she whispered. "Oh, Sam, please come back. Please. I'll make it all up to you, I really will. I swear I'll never play a trick on you again."

Jessica turned to look at the door that led to the bathroom connecting her room with her sister's. Elizabeth had been arrested. Elizabeth was in jail. Even though Jessica had played that silly joke on Elizabeth and Sam, the accident obviously had had nothing to do with Jessica. It was all Elizabeth's fault. Jessica leaned against the window frame, a smile on her lips. It was a sad smile, but it was the first time she'd smiled since the accident, so she took it as a sign. A sign that if Elizabeth was punished for Sam's death, then Jessica really would start to feel better.

"Let me out, Michelle!" begged the small,

whining voice. "Let me out! I promise I'll be good. I promise. I'll do whatever you say."

Margo sat on the floor of Georgie Smith's bedroom, her back against the closet door, humming along to Mrs. Smith's Walkman while she filed her nails. Margo frowned. Georgie was making so much noise that she couldn't concentrate. And there was something she was trying to think about. Something important she was trying to remember. That was why she really hated little kids. They never left you in peace—they were always trying to ruin things for you. If she hadn't been so desperate for money, she never would have taken this stupid baby-sitting job.

"Please!" wailed Georgie, his voice thin and shrill. "Please let me out! Michelle, I can't breathe! Michelle, I'm really scared!"

A song, that's what she was trying to remember. A song about Ohio, leaving Ohio. She had heard it on the radio a long time ago. It seemed like it must have been a long time ago. It had to be something about being so glad to leave Ohio that you could cry for joy. Leaving Ohio. The only people who wanted to stay in Ohio were stupid losers like the Smiths. No one with any brains would stay any longer than they had to. And Margo had brains. She'd been in this dumb state, in this hick town long enough. It was worse than being back on Long Island. It was even worse than most of the foster homes she'd been in. She bit her lip, ignoring the racket behind her. Ohio . . . leaving Ohio. What was it? *Oh, how I want to leave Ohio? If I don't leave Ohio I certainly will die-o?* She shook her head. She couldn't bring back the tune. The words came just to the top of her brain and then they vanished like smoke, like breath on a winter day. That happened to her a lot. She almost thought she knew something, and then—pfft!—it was gone.

Georgie started banging on the closet door again.

That little brat, Margo thought. *It's his fault. It's his fault I can't remember that song. He's really asking for it. He knows I'm thinking. He knows I'm thinking, and he's purposely trying to distract me.*

"Shut up!" Margo bellowed. "Shut up or you'll really be sorry."

Georgie started sobbing. "But, Michelle, I'm scared of the dark. And I can't breathe, Michelle. I really, really can't."

Margo tossed the used nail file across the room, took out a new one from Mrs. Smith's makeup case, and went back to her thinking. She could still remember the song about California. Even though that stupid kid was trying to upset her, trying to ruin her afternoon, she could still remember the song about California. An evil grin broke across Margo's face. California, that's where she was going.

Georgie's crying grew louder and more uncontrollable. Margo turned up the volume on the Walkman.

California was where life was perfect. In California Margo would find everything she'd ever wanted. She knew that. She knew, because her voice had told her so. *California,* the voice whispered to her every night. *California is where you want to go, Margo. California is your destiny.*

Margo blew on her nails. Not only would she make a lot of friends in California and find a good-looking California boyfriend, but California was where her real family would be. Her real family and her real life. The last sixteen years had been a mistake; she'd gotten stuck in someone else's life. She knew that. She knew that she'd been taken from her parents by an evil, hateful old witch when she was born. The voice had told her that, too. But once she got to California, everything would be all right. Everything would be straightened out. She'd heard the voice, and the voice had told her that her real home and her real life were all waiting for her underneath the golden sun and green palm trees of California. All Margo had to do was get her hands on some money and get there. But Georgie was stopping her. Georgie hadn't told her that the ring she'd stolen from his mother was fake. Georgie hadn't warned her that his parents never kept any cash in the house.

Behind her, the closet door vibrated.

Margo smiled once more. Just last night she'd overheard Mrs. Smith talking about a consignment of valuable Victorian jewelry that was coming into her antique shop in the next few days. If Margo could get her hands on that, she'd finally be able to leave. Leave the Smiths. Leave Ohio. Leave the past behind.

"Michelle!"

Georgie threw himself against the door so hard that Margo dropped the file. That did it. How much was she supposed to take? How much was she supposed to put up with? Wasn't she ever allowed to have time for anything *she* wanted?

Margo jumped to her feet and yanked open the closet door. Red and crying, his face and shirt wet with tears, Georgie rolled out.

"You little creep!" shrieked Margo. "Why can't you ever do anything you're told? Why do you always have to ruin everything for me?" She gave him a kick. Margo knew from all the times she'd been beaten herself that the best place to hit someone was in the head. You couldn't see the bruises there. You couldn't see the scars.

She kicked him again. It made her feel strong to hear him beg her to stop.

Georgie wrapped his arms around his head to try to protect himself. He was pathetic, that's what he was. Absolutely pathetic. Like a worm or a little bug you could just step on and squash. But there was something about the sight of him cowering and sniveling on the floor that made Margo feel even better. It was power. She had the power to make this cowardly little weakling do anything she wanted. And that made her feel as close to happy as Margo ever felt.

She grabbed hold of one skinny arm and pulled Georgie to his feet. "You better not tell anyone about this, you hear me, you worthless little runt?"

"Don't hit me!" the little boy begged. "Please, Michelle! Don't hit me again."

She shook him so hard she could hear his teeth knock together. "Do you promise?" she screamed. "I swear I'll kill you if you tell anyone. I'll kill you and then I'll feed you to the dogs."

"I promise, Michelle!" Georgie sobbed. "I promise. I won't tell anyone."

"And you promise you'll do whatever I say? You promise you'll help me if I need you to?"

Georgie's head was bobbing up and down. "Yes," he gasped eagerly. "Yes, I promise. I'll do whatever you want, Michelle. Just don't lock me in the closet again. Don't hit me anymore."

Margo let him go, and he dropped limply to the floor.

"Good," she said. Another smile—this one like a snake. There was a glint in those arctic eyes. *California, here I come!* she silently cried.

Chapter 2

Nicholas Morrow tightened his maroon silk tie, straightened the lapel on his blue linen suit, and smiled at himself in the hall mirror before leaving for work. "Not bad," he told his reflection. "Not bad at all. Elegant, but understated. Businesslike, but with an edge of flamboyance and originality. Just like me." He gave himself a wink. "What girl could resist a combination like that?"

The wink became a wry, self-deprecating smile. "Roughly every single woman in the state of California and one in Oregon," he answered. "At last count."

Nicholas sighed. He made jokes about the fact that he was a shoo-in to win this decade's

Loser in Love Award, but the truth was that he was beginning to find it pretty unfunny. The only woman who thought he was handsome and dashing and wonderful was Olivia Davidson, and she was his best friend, not a potential girlfriend. It was like being admired by your sister. It just didn't count, somehow.

He studied himself in the mirror. What was wrong with him? He was attractive, he was nice, he was loyal, and he was reasonably intelligent; he had a good sense of humor, a range of interests, and he even had money. He didn't drink, gamble, drive too fast, and he loved animals. Why was it that every girl he went out with either dumped him after the second date or put him to sleep?

Nicholas made a face. One of the worst had definitely been the girl from Oregon. She had spent the entire evening talking about boll weevils, or something like boll weevils, and when he had taken her home, she thanked him politely and said that she'd prefer if he didn't call her again—she didn't think he was what she was looking for. He'd had to stop himself from asking her if she was looking for someone who worked in pest control.

All Nicholas was looking for was a little companionship and affection. Someone to share things with. Was that asking so much? Other people managed to find their true loves. Why couldn't he?

"Because they can tell that you come from another planet," he informed his image. He grabbed his attache case. "It's the second head that gives it away."

He picked up the mail Nora, the housekeeper, had put on the hall table and began to sort through it. There was a letter from a friend in New York. A letter from a business acquaintance in Hawaii. A postcard from a cousin on vacation in Toronto. And a letter addressed in neon pink, with an enormous red kiss mark sealing the back flap.

Nick laughed to himself. "The mailman must be getting too much sun," he said. Convinced it must be a mistake, he turned the envelope over. But the name and address on the front were his.

He put his case on the floor and slowly opened the letter. The expression on his face changed from bewilderment to horror. It wasn't a joke. It was from *Hunks*, a popular television show that gave contestants the chance to meet the girl of their dreams.

Nicholas leaned against the wall for support and began to read.

Dear Nicholas Morrow,
Let me congratulate you on being se-

*lected to participate in "Hunks," one of
the nation's most successful game shows—
and the only one with a heart. From the
details we've received, we think you are
the ideal Hunk—handsome and hopeful
about love—and we look forward to helping you change your life and your luck.*

He read the letter three times to make sure
he'd understood it. Who could have sent his
name into the show? Who could have given
'them the "details" that convinced them he was
perfect for *Hunks*?

An affectionate smile suddenly lit up
Nicholas's good-looking face. It had to be! There
was only one person who knew him well enough
to know how lonely he really was. The smile became even brighter. And only one person who
cared about him enough to want to jolt him out
of the rut he was in, and who also had the sense
of humor to come up with something like this.

"Olivia!" Nicholas laughed out loud. There
was no one else it could be. Just to show what a
good sport he was—and how much he appreci-
ated Olivia's concern—he was going to phone
the producer as soon as he got to his office.
After all, what did he have to lose? He looked
down at the envelope. Along the bottom, in dark
red, was the legend *Dream Girls for Dream*

35

Guys. Nicholas was whistling as he walked out the door. He had nothing to lose and everything to gain.

Elizabeth glanced anxiously at her watch, waiting for the minute hand to make that last leap so the period would be over. Her books were already neatly stacked in front of her and her feet were ready to move. She checked her watch again. Twenty-two seconds to go.

Elizabeth had been convinced that there couldn't be anything worse than a night in jail. Too frightened and miserable to sleep, she'd huddled in her lonely corner, waiting for morning, listening to her cellmates' snores and the pounding of her own heart. She'd kept the tears at bay only by telling herself over and over, *All you have to do is get through this, and you'll be able to get through anything.*

But she'd been wrong. Today was her first day back at Sweet Valley High since she had been released on bail, and as far as Elizabeth was concerned, it made prison seem like a picnic on the beach. No Monday had ever looked quite so bleak.

Elizabeth was out of her seat and through the classroom door as soon as the bell rang. In the past, of course, she would have lingered after class, talking with Maria Santini or Bill

Chase, who sat on either side of her, about the homework assignment they'd just been given or her plans for the weekend. Then she would have met her best friend, Enid Rollins, outside of her math class, and together they would have strolled to the lunchroom, where Todd, Elizabeth's boyfriend, would be sitting at their usual table, waiting for her.

But that was in the past—a lifetime ago. In that life Elizabeth Wakefield had been a carefree and happy teenager, admired and liked by everyone. In this life she was a criminal, condemned by many and shunned by all.

Her head down, her eyes on the brown floor tiles, Elizabeth hurried to her locker. From the moment she had walked through the school entrance that morning, Elizabeth had felt like an outcast. Heads looked up when she entered a room, eyes followed her wherever she went. Instead of the smiles and greetings she was used to, she was met with stony faces and silence. *Well, what did you expect?* she angrily asked herself as she barreled down the hallway. *You were arrested for killing your sister's boyfriend. How did you think people would act? Like you'd just won the Nobel Peace Prize?*

All she wanted was to get to the cafeteria before it filled up. She could grab a table in the far corner of the room where no one would notice

37

her. At least it would save her the humiliation of having to walk through the crowded room, with everyone watching and talking about her.

Looking up at that moment, Elizabeth saw Enid standing outside the door of her math room. Enid started to smile at her—the first smile Elizabeth had received all morning—but instead of making Elizabeth feel better, it made her feel worse. She couldn't face Enid, not now. Right after the accident, Enid had given her valuable support. But everything was different now.

Last night Elizabeth had sat in her room, looking at pictures of herself, Todd, Jessica, and Sam all together. Those pictures had made her feel as if her heart would break. And seeing Enid waiting for her made her feel the same way. There was no getting back to the time of those photographs; there was no pretending that things hadn't changed. Trying to act as though she'd suddenly remembered something important, Elizabeth turned sharply down the hall to her right, forcing back the tears that had turned the hallways of Sweet Valley High into corridors of misery.

"You're kidding, aren't you, Amy?" Jessica Wakefield's warm, contagious laugh bubbled through the hall. "He used your silk scarf to wipe off the windshield? I would have made him use his shirt."

Amy Sutton shook her head. "I wanted to kill him, Jess, I—" Amy stopped suddenly, putting a hand over her mouth. "Oh, Jess, I'm sorry—I—"

Jessica stopped too, turning her big blue-green eyes on her friend in bewilderment. "What's the matter, Amy?" she asked innocently. "You don't have anything to be sorry about."

Amy's face was bright red. "Oh, but Sam . . . I mean, I shouldn't have joked about—"

Knowing what Amy was trying to say, Jessica cut her off as quickly as possible. "You can joke about anything you want," she said dismissively. "It doesn't bother me." Pulling her books closer to her chest, she started striding down the corridor again.

Amy hurried to keep up with her. "Really, Jess?" she asked in a hushed voice. "I mean, it's great that you seem to have recovered so quickly, but are you really all right? I mean, you've been through an awful ordeal. You must know how badly everybody feels for you."

"I know," said Jessica. The knowledge that everyone in school was sympathetic to her for a change—that they all felt sorry for what she was going through—was the one comfort Jessica had when she lay awake at night, trying to erase Sam's image from her mind so she could get some sleep. She tossed her shimmering gold hair over her shoulder. "I'm fine," she said firmly. "I'm absolutely fine." She smiled bravely and the dimple appeared in her left cheek. "I have everything under control, Amy. Really."

For once in her life, Jessica was telling the absolute truth. She did have everything under control. There was a song her father used to sing when the twins were little, to get them out of their bad moods. Jessica wasn't sure what the name of the song was or how it went, but she remembered that the refrain was something about pretending to be happy when you weren't. And that was exactly what she had decided to do. To pretend she was all right. To pretend to be fun-loving Jessica Wakefield again. For as much as she liked the fact that for once everyone was on her side and not Elizabeth's, as much as she enjoyed being the center of attention and sympathy, she didn't want anyone to get too close to her. She didn't want them to know the truth.

Jessica started to laugh again as she and Amy turned toward the cafeteria, but the laughter died in her throat. Just disappearing through the lunchroom doors was Elizabeth. Jessica's eyes darkened. All her parents talked about now was poor Elizabeth, and how their father was going to clear her name. Well, she'd see about that. Even if their father did clear Elizabeth, even if she didn't spend the rest of her life in jail where she belonged, Jessica had finally realized the one thing that would make *her* feel better. The one thing that would ease some of the pain caused by Sam's death. And that was revenge.

Jessica's hand tightened on her bag. That was the reason she was pretending to be all right. Because if anyone suspected how she really felt, they might try to stop her.

Packed as the cafeteria was, Elizabeth had a corner at the back to herself. She had a book open in front of her while she ate her lunch, so she didn't have to see either the eyes looking at her or the eyes looking away. So she wouldn't see Todd come in and sit with someone else.

Elizabeth read the same line over for the third time. She'd only seen Todd once since the accident, and that had been at Sam's funeral. For some reason, she hadn't been able to make the first move toward him. When he'd moved toward her, she'd turned away. Later, Todd had spoken to her parents, he'd put his arm around Jessica and hugged her, but he hadn't tried to approach Elizabeth again. He'd refused to meet her eyes.

Ever since then, Elizabeth had been waiting for him to phone. Every morning she'd wake up and think, *He'll call today. He was in shock be-*

fore. But today he'll call to see how I am. He can't really be mad at me. He can't really hate me. He'll call today for sure. But Todd never called.

Even this morning when she was getting ready for school Elizabeth had still dared to hope that when he saw her, Todd would act like his old self. His old, kind, understanding, and loving self. That he would come over and slip his arm through hers and tell her that he'd been worried about her. But when he saw her from the end of the hallway, he'd turned away, laughing at something someone else had said.

Elizabeth took another bite of her sandwich, even though it tasted like cardboard, and chewed it slowly. Secretly she hoped that maybe, just maybe, if Todd saw her sitting all alone, some feeling for her would tug at his heart. All through her last class, she had imagined sitting just like this, reading her book and trying to eat, and then suddenly she would feel a hand on her shoulder and it would be Todd. "This seat taken?" he'd ask her with a grin, pulling out the chair next to her. "Mind if I join you?"

A hand fell gently on Elizabeth's shoulder. She caught her breath. It was Todd. It was just as she'd hoped.

"I don't know what you think you're doing

avoiding me, Elizabeth Wakefield," said a familiar voice. "But let me tell you right now that it isn't going to work."

Elizabeth looked up, trying to hide her disappointment. It wasn't Todd after all.

Enid threw her book bag on the table. "Why did you ignore me back there?" she demanded. "You knew I was waiting for you."

Elizabeth felt herself blush. "I just—" She shook her head, but didn't move her eyes from Enid's. "I don't know," she finally admitted. "It's just so awful. I couldn't pretend it wasn't—"

"Nobody's asking you to pretend anything," Enid said. "But I'm your best friend, Elizabeth, and I'm not going to let you forget it. Is that understood?"

In spite of herself, Elizabeth found herself smiling. "Understood."

Enid smiled back. "Good." She slung her bag over her shoulder. "Now I'm going to get myself some lunch. You want anything?"

Elizabeth shook her head. "No," she said, gesturing to the food in front of her. "Thanks, I'm fine."

Elizabeth watched Enid cross the cafeteria and get in line. For the first time since the school day had begun, she was feeling a little better. At least with Enid beside her she didn't feel so alone.

She pushed her tray away and leaned back in her chair, but almost immediately she felt all eyes on her again. What could she do until Enid came back? She couldn't just sit there staring at the tabletop. Elizabeth shifted in her seat. She was as tired of pretending to read her history book as she was of pretending to eat. Glancing over, she noticed a copy of the local paper sticking out of Enid's book bag. She could read that while she waited for her friend to come back.

"Oh, no!" Elizabeth's gasp was loud enough to be heard by the group at the next table. They turned to look at her, but Elizabeth was staring at the page in front of her, transfixed by the smiling face staring back. It was a photo of her! She looked the way she used to, the week before the Jungle Prom—a happy girl with a perfect life. Elizabeth's eyes moved up. Above the smiling photo was the headline: Local Girl to Stand Trial.

Elizabeth dropped the paper as though it had burned her. Hot, bitter tears filled her eyes. How could Enid do this to her? How could she pretend to be her friend, when all along she'd obviously intended for Elizabeth to see that story?

Elizabeth got up so quickly she knocked over her chair. There was nobody on her side at Sweet Valley High. The whole world was against her. She grabbed her things from the table. She didn't have to stay here. She could go home. She could go home and never come back. Leaving the paper on the floor where it had fallen, Elizabeth raced from the cafeteria.

"My father's insisting that we take Grace to dinner at a Mexican restaurant he knows outside L.A.," Lila was saying. "But I really think she'd prefer someplace where we might run into some stars." She looked around the table at Amy, Annie Whitman, Caroline Pearce, and Jessica. "Don't you?" she asked. "I mean, she's come all the way from Paris. She'll want to see the city, not sit behind a potted cactus, eating burritos."

Annie shook her head. "I'm sure you're right," she said quickly. "She probably doesn't even like Mexican food."

Lila shook her dark hair. "I don't know why you'd say a thing like that, Annie," she said crisply. "My mother's a very sophisticated woman, you know. I'm sure she's sampled every cuisine in the world."

Amy exchanged a look with Annie that Lila didn't see. "Maybe she doesn't care where she's going to eat," Amy suggested cautiously. "Maybe she just wants to be with you."

Lila took a demure bite of her stuffed crois-sant. For the past few days she'd been going through a "continental" phase, which included a lot of croissants. "Of course she wants to be with me," she said, losing a little of her good humor. "That's not the point."

"What is the point?" Caroline muttered under her breath. "We've heard about this dinner so many times that I feel as though it's already happened and I was there with you."

Lila was still talking and didn't hear her. "The point is that I want everything to be perfect for her." She gave Amy an impatient look. "You know that, Amy," she reminded her.

Caroline shrugged. "Your mother's staying at the Beverly Hills Hotel, isn't she?" she asked. "What could be more perfect than having dinner there?"

Lila brushed back her hair. "I'm sure my mother will get bored with eating there," she said. She turned to Jessica. "What do you think, Jess?"

Jessica looked up with a start. Ever since they'd sat down to eat lunch, Lila had been talking about her mother. They'd heard ten minutes' worth of how beautiful and intelligent she was, and now they were hearing twenty minutes of what and where she liked to eat. Jessica was finding the whole thing irritating. There were more important things in life than Lila and her mother and their favorite restaurants. There was death, for instance. Jessica's eyes flicked across the room to where her sister sat, talking to Enid. And there was vengeance.

"Jessica?" Lila was holding a black olive between her fingers, and looking at her intently. "Jessica, did you hear what I said?"

Collecting herself, Jessica put on her brightest cheerleader smile. "Of course," she said lightly. She took up a large forkful of salad. "And I think you're absolutely right. Mexican *is* too ethnic for someone from Paris. She'll be used to much more elegant food."

Lila beamed at her approvingly. "You see?" she said to the others. "Jessica understands."

Jessica beamed back, but her attention was still on the almost-empty table at the other side of the cafeteria. Enid, leaving her books next to Elizabeth, was walking away. Jessica felt a thrill of triumph run up her spine. It was going to work. She'd carefully folded the paper so Enid couldn't see the front page, and then she'd quickly stuck it into Enid's book bag as Enid passed by Jessica's table.

"Well, I'm glad someone does," said Caroline sourly. "What I don't understand is why you're so anxious to meet your mother, when everyone else wishes they could get rid of their mothers for a while." She made a face. "My mother drives me crazy most of the time!"

47

"Really, Caroline!" Jessica snapped. "How insensitive can you be? Lila hasn't even *seen* her mother since she was two."

Caroline was taken aback. "I didn't mean anything," she protested, looking for support from Annie and Amy. "I was just making a little joke."

"*Little* being the operative word," said Lila.

Out of the corner of her eye, Jessica watched Elizabeth unfold the Sweet Valley paper. She saw her put her hand to her mouth. She saw the paper fall to the ground.

"Sometimes I really don't understand you, Caroline," said Jessica, turning her eyes to Lila so that she felt, rather than saw, her twin rush from the room. "You just never think of anybody but yourself, do you?" she asked.

Steven was beginning to feel like a hamster running around and around on its wheel. He got up in the morning, went to his classes, and then he came back to the apartment in the evening. Around and around he went, never stopping and never getting anywhere.

He threw his pen down on the desk in disgust. He couldn't concentrate, that was the problem. He couldn't concentrate in class, and he couldn't concentrate at home. Sometimes he found himself just standing in a room, wondering what he was doing there. Last night he discovered that he was out of milk, coffee, bread, and butter, but that the toothpaste he hadn't been able to find was in the refrigerator. This morning he'd been forced to put on the socks he'd worn yesterday because he'd forgotten—*again*—to do the laundry.

Steven leaned his head on his hands, trying to make himself think clearly. But it seemed that all he could think about was his family.

Mr. Wakefield was putting up a brave front—talking about acquittals and public apologies and how it was always darkest before the dawn—but Steven still wasn't sure what was really happening. Whenever he asked about Elizabeth and Jessica, his father always described them both as "doing as well as can be expected."

Steven sat up, tilting back in his chair. *As well as can be expected*. What was that supposed to mean? Elizabeth stood accused of involuntary manslaughter, and Jessica's boyfriend was dead. How well were they expected to do? Steven sighed. For all he knew, that meant that they were both having nervous breakdowns.

Steven stared at the phone. His mother wasn't any more help than his father. Whenever he asked *her* how things were, she said, "Oh, fine, darling. Fine. Don't you worry about us. Everything's fine."

Steven shook his head. He was beginning to think that even if the entire family were about to be carted off to jail, his mother would tell him they were fine. "Don't worry about us, darling," she'd say.

He snatched up his pen again. He was going to have to get himself together. He was going to make a list of the things he had to do. Then maybe he'd be able to stop worrying about Elizabeth and get back to his own life.

"Things to do" he wrote at the top of the pad. Shopping. Laundry. Paper for Professor Mixle. Find roommate.

Find a roommate! His father's original phone call had upset him so much that he'd completely forgotten about the ad in the paper.

Glad to have something simple to do, Steven got up and fished the newspaper out of the pile on the coffee table. "Five-five-five, one-two-three-two," he repeated out loud as he pushed the numbers.

The answering machine picked up on the fourth ring. "Neither David nor Billie is in right now," said a pleasant male voice.

"Leave a message after the tone, and we'll get right back to you."

Steven left a message. He gave his name and phone number, he described the apartment, he quoted the rent. And then, just as he was about to suggest a good time for Billie Winkler to come see it, he decided that he wouldn't be here to show it to him. He was going back to Sweet Valley for a surprise visit; to see for himself what state his family was in.

"I think I might be away this coming weekend," he said. "So why don't you come over next Monday evening if you're interested? If I don't get a message to the contrary, I'll expect you then."

Feeling happier than he had since he had first gotten the news about Elizabeth, Steven went into the kitchen to get himself a soft drink. He opened the refrigerator, staring in at the one egg and the jar of pickles that were its sole occupants.

The other good thing about going home was that he'd be fed well. He looked down at his two-day-old socks. He'd better remember to bring his laundry, too.

Margo was having a dream. She was in a closet. It was very, very dark in the closet, and she could barely breathe. Margo hated the dark. There were horrible things in the dark. Things that wanted to hurt her. That was what the voice always said. Not the voice that loved her and took care of her. The other voice. The witch's voice. The voice she always heard in her dreams.

In this dream, Margo was in the closet and the voice was outside. "I warned you, didn't I?" it asked. "Didn't I warn you, you little brat? Didn't I tell you that you better do what I said?" The voice started laughing. The voice's laugh was high and shrill. It hurt Margo's ears to hear it. Margo started to cry.

The voice became taunting. "Oh, are you crying, poor little Margo? What does poor little Margo want? Her mommy?" The voice's laughter was so loud and painful that Margo tried to put her hands to her ears. But she couldn't; her hands were tied behind her back.

"You thought you were clever, didn't you?" asked the voice. "You thought you could get away from me. You thought you could run away on those skinny little legs, and that I would never find you."

The laughter was so loud that Margo's head began to throb. She crouched in the corner, tears pouring down her face, her nose streaming, trying to get enough air to breathe. But it was so dark in the closet. So dark and so small. "Please!" Margo begged. "Please don't hurt me anymore. Please just let me out. I'll be good. I swear I will."

The voice was laughing so loudly that Margo felt as though she were inside a bell, and the sound of the laughter was all around her. "Oh, no, you don't," said the voice. "You think you'll sneak away again. I know you. You think you'll find your real family. But I *am* your real family. And I want you. I want you for myself!"

In Margo's dream, the closet door flew open and she was blinded by the sudden light. A strong arm grabbed her and yanked her out. "Let me show you what I'm going to do to you now!" said the voice. "What do you think, little Margo? What do you think I'm going to do now?"

Margo woke up screaming.

The sheet was damp with her sweat and tears.

Margo. Margo, you have to get out of here. You have to get out of here now. You have to go to California. You have to find your real home.

Still shaking and breathing heavily, Margo slowly opened her eyes. She was all right. She was safe. It was just a bad dream, and the dream was over. Her voice had found her again. Her voice was wrapping itself around her, warm and comforting. Just like a mother. And just like a mother, her voice was telling her what to do.

It's time, Margo. It's time to go. The brat knows where the keys are. The brat can show you. The keys to the safe where Mrs. Smith put those jewels, Margo. This is your chance. Your destiny is waiting for you. Your family, Margo. Your real mother. Your real father. Your real home. Don't let anything stop you, darling. Not anything. It's time to go.

Chapter 3

Jessica and Lila were leaving Sweet Valley High together on Thursday afternoon. Lila was smiling and chatting happily, but Jessica had to stop herself from looking as annoyed as she felt.

"Oh, really?" she answered vaguely to something Lila was saying. "No, I didn't know that."

The problem was that Lila was interrupting Jessica's thoughts. Jessica was trying to think about the story they'd discussed in her English class that afternoon, but Lila wanted to talk about her mother. Again.

"And did you know that Grace can fly her own plane?" Lila was saying now. "Isn't that something? I mean, she's probably so rich that she doesn't even have to drive her own car, but she flies her own plane."

"Gee," replied Jessica. "That really is great."

The English-class story had been about a woman who had waited thirty years to avenge the death of her husband. Thirty years of plotting and planning and setting everything up just right.

Lila sighed. "I just wish I could get my father to talk about her more," she went on. "But it's hard enough for him to find time to talk about the weather. And he doesn't *mind* talking about that. But when it comes to my mother, he's practically taken a vow of silence."

The best part about the story, as far as Jessica was concerned, had been that the woman's patience had paid off. After thirty years, she had finally gotten her revenge. Jessica squinted as she and Lila stepped into the afternoon sunshine. But Jessica wasn't willing to wait thirty years. She wanted her revenge right now.

"Oh, I don't believe it!" Lila's voice was between a groan and a squeal. "I completely forgot to tell you what I found in the attic. Wait'll you hear. It's the neatest thing."

The sheer volume of Lila's voice finally forced Jessica to look at her. She wanted to say *No, Lila, no you didn't tell me. And please don't bother telling me now. I have more important*

things to think about than you and your mother.
Instead she said, "What is it Lila?"

Lila hugged her books against her chest. "A picture!" The way she said it made it sound as though she'd discovered a gold credit card with no spending limit. "A picture of me and Grace!"

Jessica put what she hoped was an interested expression on her face. "Really? A picture of you and Grace? That's terrific." Lila beamed. "Uh-huh. I must be about a year old in the picture. We're sitting together on a sofa."

"Wow," said Jessica. "You're sitting on a sofa. That's incredible."

Lila came to a sudden stop. "Are you making fun of me, Jessica Wakefield?" she demanded. "Because if you are, I want you to know that I don't think it's funny at all. Meeting my mother happens to be very important to me."

Jessica stopped too. *You think that's important?* she wanted to scream. *You think that's important? Well, I'll tell you what I think is important! I think it's important that Sam's dead! I think it's important that I'll never see him again as long as I live. I'll never get to tell him how sorry I am for what I—for what happened! I think it's important that somebody pays for Sam's death, that's what I think's important!*

"Well?" Lila was tapping her foot. "Are you making fun of me?"

Somehow, Jessica managed to keep the anger inside, and not let the smile slip from her lips or the tears spill out of her eyes.

"Of course I'm not making fun of you," she said soothingly. "I think it's great that you're finally getting to meet your mom."

Several yards behind Lila, Todd Wilkins was crossing the parking lot by himself, looking like he hadn't a friend in the world. Jessica's anger vanished and a feeling of calm and certainty took its place. Todd! Why hadn't she thought of Todd before?

Lila made a face. "I know I'm a little obsessive about her," she apologized. "But I'm so excited . . . I just can't help myself."

But I can help myself, thought Jessica. *I can help myself, get my revenge*—and *not have to wait thirty years*.

Jessica and Lila weren't the only ones with a lot on their minds that afternoon. Bruce Patman had a lot on his mind too. What he had on his mind was about five foot eight, slender and dark, with eyes as blue as the sky.

Bruce flicked a button on the TV remote and changed the channel. He didn't want to think about those eyes. He closed his own eyes but he could still see them, staring at him, pleading with him. From the eyes it only took a fraction of a second to reach those full, soft lips.

Bruce opened his eyes and changed the channel again. He didn't want to think about those lips, either. He didn't want to think about Pamela Robertson at all. What he wanted was to forget her. To forget that he ever knew she existed.

Suddenly he found himself looking into the face of a smiling young woman. A smiling young man was handing her a bouquet of roses. The young woman in the commercial looked nothing like Pamela and the young man looked nothing like Bruce. But the flowers were almost identical to the bouquet he'd bought for Pamela that dreadful morning after their second date. The young man and young woman were gazing into each other's eyes. He could remember looking at Pamela like that. He could remember thinking, *So this is love.* What a complete jerk he was. Where other people had brains, all he had was an empty space.

Something got into his eyes, making them water. He brushed the tears away on the sleeve of his shirt.

"Don't let her fool you!" Bruce shouted at the television. "She's only going to break your heart! Take it from me, man. Anybody who falls in love deserves what he gets."

He snapped off the TV and hurled the remote across the room. How was he supposed to forget about Pamela when everything was conspiring to make him remember? When he went to school, he remembered the first time he had seen her, on the football field. When he drove around Sweet Valley, he remembered driving to Big Mesa to find her, and the first time she had sat beside him in the passenger seat. When he got into bed at night and looked out at the sky, he remembered all the plans he'd had for them, all the dreams. Now he couldn't even watch a commercial without being reminded of her. The entire world was pitted against him.

Bruce slumped on the oversize white leather sofa of the den, willing himself to think of something else—tennis, the new café at the country club, all the beautiful girls in California who would give their perfect tans for a date with someone as wealthy and handsome as he. But still Pamela stole her way into his mind. Maybe he had overreacted. Maybe he should have given her an opportunity to explain. Maybe he should give her another chance. Just because there was that gossip about her . . . He threw a cushion after the remote. It wasn't just gossip. He'd seen her coming home in the early morning with another boy. He'd seen it with his own eyes. There was no explanation for that. He'd thought Pamela was his angel, but she'd turned out to be a tramp.

The telephone next to the couch began to ring. It was easier to answer it than to go on thinking about Pamela.

"Hello?" Much to his relief, his voice had all of its usual casual confidence. There was no way the person on the other end of the line would ever guess what turmoil his mind was really in.

"Bruce?"

Her voice came through the receiver like a steel blade, and went straight to his heart.

"Bruce, please don't hang up. Please listen for just a minute."

He would have hung up, only he couldn't move. He had to put all his energy into keeping his heart in his chest.

"Bruce? Bruce, are you still there?"

There was no casual confidence in his voice now. "Yes, I'm still here."

He could hear Pamela take a deep breath before she began to speak. When she did speak, though, her voice was slow and gentle.

"I know you're angry," she said simply. "And I don't blame you, but I think you should give me a chance to tell you my side."

By staring at the small yellow flower on the oriental rug in front of the fireplace, Bruce managed to answer. "I don't really think you have anything to say that I want to hear."

"Listen to me," she pleaded. "Meeting you

61

changed my life. Changed me. All the things you told me about Regina and her death . . . and how meeting me had started you feeling again . . ."

Bruce wished he could close his ears against her words as easily as he could close his eyes against his own tears. But it was true; he had told her about Regina and how her death had devastated him, how he'd thought he would never really feel anything again. Until he met Pamela.

"Bruce," she said urgently. "Bruce, if there was any truth in that, then you have to give me a chance to explain. We both deserve that much."

He thought he was going to say no. "All right," he heard his voice say, still struggling for control. "I'll meet you tomorrow at eight at the Box Tree."

"Eight o'clock at the Box Tree," Pamela repeated. "I'll see you then." Then she added in almost a whisper, "Thank you, Bruce."

Later that night when he was falling asleep, he would still hear that whisper in his head, *Thank you, Bruce.*

Todd sat at his desk in his bedroom on Thursday evening. If anyone had come in just then and asked him what he was doing, he would have said that he was writing his history paper. His typewriter was in front of him, with his notes and a clean stack of paper.

But in fact, Todd wasn't writing his history paper, unless getting his name, the class, the date, and the title on the page counted.

Todd was staring at the keyboard, thinking about Elizabeth.

He felt as if he was in one of those dreams where you start walking down the same street you always walk down, but as you go farther and farther you suddenly realize that it isn't the same street at all. And when you turn to go back, there is no going back. Sometimes you can see all your friends, just a few feet away from you, but you can't touch them.

Todd groaned out loud. The worst thing was that it was all his own fault. Somehow, since the accident, he had let his life become a nightmare. He had let himself go farther and farther down the wrong street.

Even though he and Jessica had been the first to arrive at the crash after the police, he hadn't been able to react. He hadn't cried, or screamed, or done any of the usual things. He'd just stood there with Jessica crumpled against him, staring at the twisted wreckage, numb. And afterward he still hadn't really talked about it with anyone. He'd just shut it out completely, even that moment when he had thought Liz was dead. But whenever he closed his eyes at night, he saw the flashing lights of the police cars and smelled the accident again, the mingled odors of gasoline and blood.

Todd put his head in his hands. When Elizabeth had needed him the most, he hadn't been there for her. Why? Why hadn't he gone to Elizabeth right then? Why hadn't he called her the next day? Why hadn't he spoken to her at Sam's funeral? Why, why, why?

Todd raised his head and leaned back in his chair. He'd been so shocked by Sam's death, and so shocked by the way Elizabeth had been behaving at the Jungle Prom—by her running off with Sam like that—that it was as though he'd frozen inside. And now that he was beginning to thaw at last, it was too late.

He could see Elizabeth, but he couldn't touch her. He didn't know how to reach her anymore. He had gone down the wrong road and now he couldn't get back.

The phone began to ring, and it was with a feeling of relief that Todd hurried to answer it. Even if it was someone wanting to sell him a magazine subscription, at least it would keep him from thinking about Elizabeth for a few minutes.

"Wilkins's home, may I help you?"

A sweet, familiar voice poured itself through the line. "Hello, Todd?"

Todd felt as though he had swallowed his heart. It was Elizabeth! She sounded sad, but it was she. It was Elizabeth, and she had spoken his name.

He couldn't keep the tremble of excitement out of his voice. "Elizabeth?" he asked. "Liz, is that you?"

"No, Todd. It's Jessica."

Jessica? His disappointment was even greater than his joy had been. He didn't want to speak to Jessica. He couldn't remember if Jessica had ever phoned him before. It wasn't as though they'd ever been close friends. And besides, it was Elizabeth who should have been calling and turning to him now.

"Oh, Todd . . ." Jessica's voice broke and released a torrent of tears. "Oh, Todd," she gasped, "it's just so awful. . . ."

The first thought to leap into his mind was that something had happened to Elizabeth. He forced himself not to panic.

"Jessica," he said calmly. "What's wrong?" He wasn't sure if she could hear him, she was sobbing so hard. "Jessica? Try to control yourself. Take some deep breaths. . . ."

He could hear her following his instructions, gulping for air. "There," he said soothingly when the tears had finally subsided. "That's a little better. Now tell me what's wrong."

"Everything," she said in a choked voice. "I didn't know if I should call you or not, but—but I really didn't know who else to turn to. I've never felt so alone in my life."

It wasn't until he realized that this phone call had nothing to do with Elizabeth that Todd noticed he'd been holding his breath.

"I feel as though there's no point to anything," Jessica was saying. "I miss Sam so much, Todd. And everybody . . . all my friends . . . well, they're only interested in themselves. After the funeral, they acted like everything was back to normal. But things won't ever be normal for me. . . ." A fresh wave of tears washed out her words.

"Jessica . . . Jessica, please." *Talk about only being interested in yourself,* Todd thought. He'd spent the days since the accident thinking about Elizabeth and thinking about himself, but he hadn't given more than a few seconds to wondering how Jessica might feel. "You're not doing yourself any good, Jess," he said gently. "Just try to calm down a little. I'm here. I'm listening."

"No one's here," said Jessica in a hushed, unsteady voice. "Just me. I'm here all by myself. And I'm so miserable, Todd. I—I just don't know what to do."

Todd had never felt that he had much in common with Jessica, but her loneliness struck a chord in him. Liz was so far away from him now that it was almost as though *she* were dead. Maybe Jessica had been right to call him. Maybe he was the one person who really could understand how she felt.

"Hey, I've got an idea," said Todd brightly. "Why don't we go see a movie?"

Jessica sniffled. "A movie? You and me?"

"Yeah, why not? It'll do us both good to get out. And then afterward we can go get a pizza or something, and talk some more."

Jessica sniffled again. "You really want to do this?" she asked. "You really want to take me out?"

Todd frowned. He hadn't really thought of it as taking her out. He'd thought of it as going to a movie and for pizza together. But of course, Jessica didn't mean *going out* in the sense of a date. She just meant going out.

"Of course I mean it," he said quickly, a little afraid that her tears might start again. "How about tomorrow? Tomorrow night at eight."

Jessica blew her nose. "OK," she said, sounding at least a little bit better. "It's a date."

Todd didn't hear her last sentence. He was too busy thinking about Elizabeth. Maybe if he helped Jessica, he would be able to make contact with her sister again.

"How do I look?" Nicholas asked as he and

Olivia stopped in front of the entrance to the *Hunks* studio. All of a sudden he was so nervous, he was sure he must be shaking. Until they had actually arrived in L.A., not only had he not been nervous, he hadn't really believed that this was happening. It had all been so fast. One day he was answering the letter from *Hunks*, and the next he had passed his interview and was being brought in as a substitute for a contestant who had come down with the flu.

Olivia brushed his lapels and straightened his tie. "Oh, for heaven's sake, Nick," she said with a laugh. "You're just going to be on national television. What are you getting so nervous about?"

"Thank you, Olivia," Nicholas said, trying to get a glimpse of his reflection in the glass door. Maybe he should have gotten his hair cut after all. "You're very comforting. I'm really glad I brought you along for moral support."

"Stop being so melodramatic." Olivia slipped her arm through his. "You look great and you know it, Nicholas Morrow," she said. "Besides, they won't let you near a camera before you've gone through makeup." She gave him a squeeze. "I hear they can make anybody look good."

A few hours later Nicholas sat under the bright television lights, trying not to notice how many cameras were trained on him or how big the audience was. Instead, he was gazing across the space separating him from his fellow contestants.

Someone shouted, "Seven minutes!"

Nicholas's stomach lurched. He couldn't decide which made him more nervous: the thought of appearing on television as a "hunk" or the thought of having to go out with one of the "dream girls."

Making every effort not to stare, he glanced over at Dream Girl number one, whose name was Jakki. She probably wouldn't notice if he did stare at her, he reasoned. She was probably used to it. And not because she was a raving beauty, though she was probably pretty enough—beneath the purple eyeshadow and the blue lipstick were fine features and large gray eyes. She had high cheekbones and a tiny butterfly tattooed below one eye. Nicholas could almost make out a slender body underneath the baggy black dress, black leggings, ripped black lace tights, and black boots. But it was hard to imagine what she'd look like in normal clothes, with pink lips and just a little color on her face and around her eyes. It was like trying to imagine Dracula without the cape and the fangs.

Nicholas crossed his legs, suddenly uncomfortable. It was also hard to imagine what it would be like going to a restaurant with her. What kind of food would she eat? Raw meat? Bugs?

Dream Girl number two, Susan, wasn't much better. In her floral dress, pink sandals, and rather demure makeup, she actually looked very nice. If you saw her passing on the street, you'd probably think to yourself, *Now she looks like a nice, normal teenage girl.* But you'd be wrong. Somewhere in Susan's family a hyena had gotten loose. Susan couldn't stop giggling. Every time Nicholas looked over at her, or one of the other girls said something to her, or a crew member said something to someone else, Susan giggled. They'd been sitting onstage for at least thirty minutes now, and for about twenty-eight of them Susan had been giggling. It was a sound somewhere between an air leak and a hiccup.

Buddy, the show host, strode across the stage with his hands in the air. "OK, lucky contestants," he said. "We're just doing one more little test for sound and then we'll be ready to go."

Nicholas's eyes moved to Ann, Dream Girl number three. She was wearing blue and she wasn't laughing, which gave her an advantage over the other two. In fact, the only obvious thing wrong with Ann was that she seemed so embarrassed by the whole thing. Nicholas couldn't help wondering if she'd lost a bet or something.

Ann caught him looking at her and immediately turned away, an unmistakable tinge of scarlet coloring her face.

Great, Nicholas thought as the sound man nodded and Buddy took his place in the center of the stage. *There's only one of them you could actually go out in public with, and she's so shy you can't even look at her without making her blush.*

The cameras started to roll, and Nicholas sat up straight, his eyes scanning the audience for Olivia. Somehow or other he was going to have to pay her back for this.

Jessica hung up the phone and lay back on her bed. She'd done it! She knew she could, and she had. She'd gotten Todd Wilkins to ask her out. It had been even easier than she'd thought. Now all she had to do was wrap him around her little finger and convince him that he'd been dating the wrong twin all along. And that wouldn't be very hard at all.

Jessica closed her eyes for a second as fresh tears surfaced. *Don't be mad at me, Sam,* she begged silently. *Please don't be mad at me. I'm not really interested in Todd. I just want to make Elizabeth jealous. I just want to hurt her the way she hurt us.* Her body shaking with sobs, Jessica rolled over and buried her face in her pillow. "I just want to take Todd away from her the way she took you from me," she wailed out loud.

Amy yawned with boredom. She and Lila had been in The Turn of the Nail for over an hour already. Lila's nails had been transformed into elegant daggers the color of the dress she'd finally decided to wear to meet her mother the following day. It had taken half an hour just to find the exact shade of polish Lila wanted.

Lila studied her right hand while Tina, the manicurist, worked busily on her left. "I'm a little worried about the solid purple," she said to Amy. "Maybe I should have gone for two colors, or some sort of design."

Amy gave an exaggerated groan. If Lila talked about nails any more, Amy would go crazy. "I'm worried about Jessica," she said, trying to change the subject. "I think she's taking Sam's death harder than we thought. Don't you think she's been acting kind of strange lately?"

"No, I don't." Lila held her finished hand up to the light. "In fact, considering all she's been through, I think she's being incredibly normal."

"That's exactly what I mean," said Amy. "She's *too* normal. You'd think nothing had happened, the way she's bouncing around." Amy frowned at her own reflection in the hand-shaped mirror on the wall. "I've seen people more upset because their turtle died."

"Oh, don't be ridiculous," Lila said dismissively. "If there were something wrong, Jess would tell me, wouldn't she? I *am* her best friend." She wiggled her fingers as though checking to see that they worked. "I'm sure you're worrying over nothing. She's doing just fine." Lila peered at her pinky. "Unlike this nail," she said sharply. "Tina, it's smeared a little!"

Amy sighed. *When would Jessica have had a chance to tell Lila if something were wrong?* she wondered. *The only time she's not preoccupied with her mother is when she's asleep. And then she probably dreams about her.*

"No, Margo," said Georgie stubbornly. "I'm not coming out till my mommy comes home."

Margo leaned closer to the little creep's bedroom door. "Why not, sweetheart?" she asked. Her voice was so gentle it almost sounded as if she were singing. "Why won't you come out and play with me?"

"Because."

"Because why?" She could sound as soothing as honey when she wanted. As soothing as honey, and as sweet as honey too. She could sound like an angel when she wanted, like the nicest, kindest, most loving person on earth. That was how you got them to trust you. They didn't have to trust you for long.

"Just because," said Georgie.

"But you know I wasn't going to hurt you, little Georgie. You know Michelle would never hurt you. I was just playing. That's the way you play tag where I come from."

"I'm not coming out," Georgie repeated. "Not till my mommy comes home."

Margo's dark eyes narrowed. Margo planned to have stolen the Victorian jewelry and be headed west on a Greyhound by the time Georgie's mommy came home. And she didn't like having to change her plans. The trouble was that though she knew Mrs. Smith had hidden the jewels in the safe behind the family portrait in the living room, she hadn't been able to find the key. And Georgie wouldn't tell her, because his mommy had made him promise not to tell anybody.

Margo smiled at the door as the snake might have smiled at Eve. He would tell her. One way or another.

"You won't come out even for chocolate-chip cookies?" she asked. "Chocolate-chip cookies and chocolate milk?" She knew Georgie's weakness for chocolate-chip cookies and chocolate milk. It was always a mistake to have a weakness.

"But you're going to hurt me," said Georgie.

"Double-chocolate-chip with chocolate icing," said Margo. "Your favorite. And then you know what else we can do? Tomorrow we can have a picnic down at the lake. You'd like a picnic, wouldn't you, Georgie? A picnic with all your favorite things?"

"Do you promise you won't hurt me?" asked Georgie. "Do you promise you won't hurt me again?"

"Of course I promise," cooed Margo. "I was just playing before. I was playing tag."

"What will we have besides chocolate-chip cookies?" asked Georgie. She could tell that his hand was on the door.

"Peanut butter and jelly sandwiches," said Margo. "Potato chips."

"What about cheese crackers?"

Margo stood up, leaning against the wall in a position so that when Georgie came out she'd be able to grab him before he realized his mistake. It was a trick she'd learned from one of her first foster homes.

"Of course you can have cheese crackers," said Margo. "And pretzels, too."

Margo caught her breath as she heard the lock turn and saw the door slowly open. Georgie stepped into the hallway.

Margo quickly slammed the door behind him and grabbed him by the arm.

"You said you wouldn't hurt me!" Georgie howled.

"I'm not hurting you," said Margo, her voice still sweet. "I'm just holding you by the arm." *Getting ready to hurt you if you don't do what I want.*

She gave him a shake. Already the stupid little brat was starting to cry.

"You promised," Georgie wailed. "You promised you wouldn't hurt me."

Margo put her red lips close to his ear. "I won't hurt you, Georgie Porgie," she whispered. "Just tell me where your mother keeps the key to the safe."

"But I promised—"

Margo twisted his pudgy little arm just enough to let him know how much it might possibly hurt if he didn't tell her what she wanted to know. "I won't tell on you, Georgie," said Margo. "You know you can trust me." She twisted his arm just a little more.

"O—OK," Georgie stammered. "OK, Michelle. I'll tell."

Margo smiled. "Thank you, Georgie," she said. "Thank you very, very much."

He really is too stupid to live, she thought as Georgie led the way to the place where the key was hidden. *Too stupid to live.*

Chapter 4

Lila played her father's message on the answering machine after school on Friday while she brushed her hair.

"I'm going to have to work a little later than I thought tonight, sweetheart," said her father's voice. "So why don't you meet me at the office around seven thirty, and we'll leave from there?"

Lila threw the brush on her bed with a sigh. She'd been hoping that her father would come home early for a change, and that they might even have a chance to talk a little more about Grace before the reunion. But no. Her father couldn't even spare her a little extra time tonight, of all nights.

Lila wiped her sweating palms on the bed-spread. She was so nervous and frightened that she almost felt sick to her stomach. What if everything went disastrously wrong? What if she ordered the wrong thing, or spilled her water, or couldn't think of anything to say?

She got up and took her dress down from the back of the closet door. What if her mother didn't like what she was wearing? What if her mother didn't like *her?*

She slipped the purple sheath over her head. That's why she'd been hoping that her father would come home early. So he could reassure her. She'd ridden with her father enough to know that there'd be little chance of talking to him on the way to L.A. He'd probably spend the whole time on his car phone.

Lila zipped up the dress and stepped in front of her full-length mirror, a critical frown on her pretty face. She looked lovely. She turned to the left and then to the right. Yes, she really did look lovely. Despite the queasiness in her stomach, her eyes were sparkling and there was a natural glow in her cheeks. She looked like a daughter you could be proud of; like a daughter you couldn't help but love.

It's going to be all right, she thought. *It's not going to matter anymore that Daddy never has any time for me. Because now I'll have Grace.*

As she hurried downstairs and out to the car, Lila began to imagine the moment when she and her mother would actually meet. Her mother would already be at their table in the hotel dining room. She'd be dressed in black, and wearing diamonds. She would look very calm and beautiful, but she'd be playing nervously with her napkin. As soon as she saw Lila, she'd jump to her feet.

Lila slid into her lime-green Triumph and started the engine. No, maybe her mother wouldn't be waiting at the table. She would come in after Lila and her father were already seated. She'd stand in the entrance to the restaurant, looking slowly around the room from one person to the next, until finally her eyes met Lila's. It wouldn't be until she took her in her arms that Lila would see the tearstains on her cheek.

Lila began to back out of the driveway. Just as she was about to come out into the road, a motorcycle roared by, causing her to slam on the brakes.

"You lunatic!" Lila shouted after the helmeted driver. "What's the matter? Don't you think your date will wait?"

If the motorcycle rider's date had had a choice, he probably wouldn't have waited. Right at that moment, in fact, he was at home looking at his watch and saying a silent prayer. *Please,* he was pleading, *please don't let her turn up all in black. Let her have on a white blouse or something. Let her wear shoes instead of work boots.*

Nicholas looked down at his own brown shoes and his dark green slacks. How were you supposed to dress when you were going on a date with someone who looked like an extra in *Night of the Living Dead?*

Even though this was supposed to be a "special" date, he hadn't bought her flowers. The only appropriate flower he could think of was the Venus's flytrap, and he doubted that many florists in Sweet Valley stocked it. He'd also decided to dress casual since there was no way he could take Jakki Phillips to a fancy restaurant. The maitre d' would think they'd come to rob the place or something, and stop them at the door.

He glanced at himself in the mirror over the mantel. Instead of a button-down shirt, he'd put on a long-sleeved blue T-shirt, but even then he knew that he could never dress casual enough to look as though he belonged with someone like Jakki.

"Where are you going to take her?" he asked his reflection. "The cemetery?" It was too bad no one had ever thought of opening a café in a crypt.

At the thought of where he and Jakki were actually going to spend this "special" evening, Nicholas's heart sank a little lower. A movie had seemed like a good idea—movie theaters were at least mercifully dark—but the only films playing locally were lighthearted comedies. He couldn't really imagine Jakki, with her butterfly tattoo on her cheek, thinking a movie about a couple who move to the suburbs from New York City and can't get the lawn sprinkler to work was funny.

And anyway, he'd still have to take her somewhere afterward. A shudder ran through him as he imagined walking into the Dairi Burger with Jakki in tow. She didn't look like a girl who drank malteds. She looked like a girl who drank blood.

He glanced at his watch again. Maybe she wasn't coming. A little ripple of hope raced through his heart. What a stroke of luck! Maybe she'd decided he was too dull and boring for her, and was standing him up!

But then he remembered her saying that she was looking forward to their date because she'd never been out with someone who wore suits before. His hopes vanished. She was coming; she was just coming slowly. Probably she didn't believe in punctuality.

Nicholas went over to wait at the window. It

had been Jakki's idea to come to his house to pick him up. "I don't like these conventions that say the boy always has to pick up the girl," she'd told him. "I like to break the rules."

He stared glumly at the circular drive. Nicholas didn't like breaking the rules. He didn't enjoy even bending them a little. He was an ordinary, quiet kind of guy, that was what he was. A guy who wanted an ordinary, quiet life.

All of a sudden the Morrows' dogs came running up the driveway, barking and howling. Something must have upset them, but what?

Nicholas raced to the door and flung it open just as something large and black, belching smoke and spitting dirt, raced across the well-tended grass like a creature running from hell. He was still trying to figure out what it was when the driver pulled back on the rear wheel and lifted the front of the bike in the air.

The dogs went crazy.

"A wheelie," Nicholas heard himself mutter. "She's doing a wheelie on my lawn!"

Jakki lifted her visor. "You ready?" she called over the roar of the engine. She nodded behind her. "Hop on. I have a great night planned for us. We're gonna have a blast!"

Too stunned to protest, Nicholas shut the door behind him and walked slowly toward the bike. What was his problem? Why did he have such awful luck with women? He was searching for the girl of his dreams, and what did he find?

Nicholas looked at Jakki, who grinned at him as she handed him his helmet.

He found the Bride of Dracula, that's what he found.

That wasn't Nick Morrow, was it? Bruce Patman asked himself as someone with his friend's clothes and general build waved forlornly from the back of a passing motorcycle.

Bruce shook his head. No, it couldn't have been Nicholas. Nicholas wasn't the type of guy to ride on a bike. And anyway, he had a Jeep. Why would he be hitching rides with some biker when he had a Jeep?

Bruce turned his car toward town. *I'm hallucinating, that's what's happening,* he decided. *It's the stress. It's because I'm a nervous wreck.*

Even Bruce had to laugh. The idea that he, Sweet Valley's wealthiest, most sought-after, most confident, and most handsome boy, should be so torn apart over a girl was funny. Especially a girl like Pamela, he reminded himself. A girl with no self-respect.

He slowed down as he approached a light. Maybe he was wrong about what he'd seen that Sunday morning. Maybe the gossip he'd heard about her wasn't true. She did have the kindest eyes. She was warm and caring. She made him feel better than he'd ever felt before.

Bruce hit the steering wheel with his hands as he waited for the light to change. "Stop it!" he ordered himself. "You've got to stop torturing yourself like this!"

Ever since he'd agreed to meet Pamela, his thoughts had been going back and forth like a pendulum. One minute he wanted nothing to do with her, and the next he was defending her. One minute he was convinced that what everyone had told him about Pamela was true, and the next he was convinced that he'd made a terrible mistake, reacting as he had, and that he'd be lucky if she ever spoke to him again. Back and forth, back and forth. He'd gone through his afternoon classes on automatic while silently debating whether he should take Pamela something, like flowers or candy. Yes, he'd decided in math. He should take her flowers, just as a gesture. No, he'd decided in history. He shouldn't take her anything. She should be glad he was even taking himself. Definitely no, he'd decided in science lab. What did he want to give her a present for? Breaking his heart? And then, right after school, he'd driven straight into town and bought a single red rose.

As the light turned green, Bruce picked up the rose from the passenger seat and tossed it out the window. *What a dumb thing to do,* he thought angrily. *Don't be a complete fool,* he told himself. *Have some pride.*

He was still muttering to himself when he noticed a familiar car coming toward him. It was Steven Wakefield's.

Bruce frowned. "I wonder what Steven's doing here?" He'd heard from Maria Santini, whose father was a close friend of Ned Wakefield's, that Mr. Wakefield was trying to keep his son away from Sweet Valley for a while. He thought Steven was too volatile, and that his presence might do more harm than good for Elizabeth.

Bruce honked his horn as Steven passed him, but Steven didn't even slow down.

Whew, thought Bruce as he headed to the Box Tree. *And I thought I had problems. I think that must have been the most worried expression I've ever seen.*

Steven was too busy wondering what his father was going to say when he arrived home even to realize that he'd just passed Bruce. Steven made a face.

He knew exactly what his father was going to say. "Go back to school, Steven. Everything's under control. We don't need you here."

Steven knew this because his father had said

it to him both last night and this morning.

"Steven, please," his father had said. "Your mother and I would be a lot happier if we knew that at least one of our children was leading a normal life right now."

Not that he hadn't tried to argue with his father. He'd pointed out that he was being excluded from the family when they needed him most. He tried to explain how concerned he was about his sisters.

"I know you're worried about them," his father had said. "But believe me, they're fine. They're just fine."

Steven shook his head. How could they be fine when one sister was going to be standing trial for involuntary manslaughter and the other's boyfriend was dead.

The music on the radio ended and the news came on. Steven turned it off immediately. He hadn't been able to listen to the news or even look at a paper since he had heard about Elizabeth—he was afraid of hearing or seeing something about her that would make his blood boil.

And that, of course, was the real reason his father didn't want him in Sweet Valley. Mr. Wakefield probably thought Steven had too much of a temper and that he might upset people. He was probably afraid that Steven would argue with the hotshot lawyer he'd hired.

"You know what you're like," his father had told him just this morning. "You might be a brilliant lawyer yourself someday, but you'll never be a diplomat."

Steven ran a hand through his hair. His poor parents. Here he was upset because his father was trying to spare him some of the pain and turmoil the family was going through. But who knew what his father was going through? Or his mother? Thinking about his mother made him bite his lip. *What did she do to deserve any of this?* he wondered. He could see her clearly, standing in front of him, staring at him in horror.

Suddenly he realized that it wasn't his mother standing in front of him, staring at him in horror. It was a young woman who obviously hadn't been paying attention to the traffic light and had stepped in front of his car. The expression on her face was one of stunned disbelief. Steven stepped on the brakes so hard that they squealed.

The girl gave him a grateful smile and quickly stepped back onto the pavement.

Pamela was still breathing heavily when the lights changed in her favor and she could finally cross the road.

You could have been killed, she told herself

angrily. *You weren't even looking where you were going; you just charged off the curb without even thinking.*

She looked at her watch again. She was already late to meet Bruce, and she knew he wouldn't wait forever. He probably wouldn't wait more than a few minutes, which was why she was in such a hurry. He'd made it clear that there was little she could say that would make him change his mind, but she had to try.

"I have to convince him," she said to herself as she walked quickly toward the Box Tree. "I just have to make him see that it wasn't what he thinks." Besides, she had a piece of surprise news that she wanted to tell him before someone else did.

Worry wrapped itself around Pamela like a heavy blanket. Bruce might think he knew her reputation, but she also knew his. Love 'Em and Leave 'Em Patman. Mr. Big Man with the Big Ego and No Heart. She laughed to herself, a sharp and bitter laugh. Her whole life was a mess because of a boy who everyone thought of as a selfish jerk. A boy not unlike Bruce Patman.

At the thought of Jake Jacoby, a look of disgust clouded her blue eyes. She'd dated Jake for several months last year, and had been convinced that she was in love with him. He had said he was in love with her, too—and therefore they should go all the way. Pamela hadn't wanted to. When she refused, he had thrown her out of the car and had never spoken to her again.

He spoke to everyone else, though. He told all his friends that she was easy. As far as Pamela knew, he'd probably told complete strangers as well. All of a sudden she was the most popular girl at Big Mesa. Even the most popular boys started asking her out. But they only asked her out once. When they realized that she wouldn't do what they wanted, they dropped her like a hot potato. They kept the rumors going, though. They kept them going and they even added to them. None of them wanted to think he was the only one who couldn't score, so they all lied. Soon even Pamela's best friends began to wonder about her. "There's no smoke without fire," she heard them whisper. "It's her word against theirs, and there are a lot more of them."

That's why she'd gone out with Jake on Saturday night. To make him stop the gossip. To beg him to do something to restore her reputation.

Jake had actually laughed at her. "What do you think I'm gonna do?" he demanded. "Make a public apology?" He'd practically choked with laughter. "You want me to tell everybody that a girl who said she was in love with me would only let me kiss her?"

And then came the crowning blow. "I'll do something for your reputation," he told her. "I'll keep you here all night and ruin it once and for all."

Pamela crossed her fingers as she stood at the corner across from the Box Tree Café, waiting for the one car coming down the road to pass. "Please," she whispered. "Please let Bruce believe me. Then I'll be able to tell him my news."

Todd wasn't sure how he had gotten himself into this situation—going to a movie with Jessica when he was missing Elizabeth so much. The more he thought about it, the more worried he became. Jessica didn't exactly hate him, but she'd never made any secret of the fact that she thought he was pretty dull and boring.

Todd put on his signal for a left-hand turn. Out of the corner of his eye, he saw a car just like Mrs. Wakefield's parked on the other side of the street. There was something red on the hood, but he went by too fast to make out what it was.

There was one question that kept nagging at him. Why would Jessica turn to him in her hour of need, when Elizabeth, who needed him more, wouldn't come near him?

He pulled into the parking lot. At least he

hadn't let Jessica talk him into meeting her at the Wakefield house. How would he have faced Mr. and Mrs. Wakefield? A cold chill swept through his body as he shut off the engine. How would he have faced Elizabeth?

I hope I'm doing the right thing, Todd thought as he got out of the car. *At least it's a start. If I'm talking to Jessica, then sooner or later I'll have to talk to Elizabeth.*

This afternoon, seeing Jessica laughing and chatting with her friends across the cafeteria, he'd suddenly had the idea that she'd only lured him out with her because she was trying to get him and Elizabeth back together. It was the sort of scheme that had Jessica's name written all over it. She'd get him to ask her out, and then when he got to the movies, instead of Jessica standing there waiting for him, it would be Elizabeth.

Todd's pace quickened as he reached the front of the movie theater. He knew it was ridiculous, but what if this really was one of Jessica's schemes?

He caught his breath as he saw her standing in front of the building, her hair looking like poured gold, those blue-green eyes looking up and down the street. Looking for him.

Todd's heart nearly broke through his chest. *It is Elizabeth,* he thought, weak with joy. *It really is!*

"Todd!" She waved. "Todd, over here."

Todd's pulse and respiration went back to normal. He grinned back. "Hi, Jess," he called. "I'm sorry I'm a little late."

Jessica ran up and slipped her arm through his. "Better late than never," she said with a smile.

Complaining of a headache, Elizabeth left her mother picking out scented soaps and went back to wait in the car.

Mrs. Wakefield had insisted on driving Elizabeth into town to do some shopping. "You really haven't been out in days," she'd argued. "Why don't you let me take you into town and buy you something special?"

Because I don't want anything, Elizabeth had wanted to answer. *Because I don't deserve anything.*

Her mother's smile had become even brighter and more determined. "I know what! There's a new Thai restaurant at the mall that everyone says is terrific. Why don't we do some shopping and then go there for a bite?"

Actually Elizabeth didn't care if she ever ate again, but seeing how hard her mother was trying, she finally relented. And besides, she'd told herself, maybe her mother was right, and it would do her good to get out.

Elizabeth approached the street where the car was parked. It hadn't done her any good at all. Everywhere she went she was sure people were staring at her and whispering. "Isn't that Elizabeth Wakefield? Isn't that the girl who killed her sister's boyfriend?"

Just as Elizabeth reached the corner, she saw Todd drive by. Her heart began to beat so fast that it hurt. *I wonder where he's going?* she asked herself. And then she answered herself. *It's Friday night. Where do you think he's going? He probably has a date.*

Elizabeth stumbled toward the car. She had to get inside before she broke down completely. She started to open the door, then she noticed something on the hood. It was a single red rose. She picked it up tenderly and held it in her open palm as the tears began to fall and fall.

Margo sat back in her seat with a contented sigh. The bus was only half full, and there was no else in the back, so she could relax.

She quietly reached into her old blue tote bag and removed her treasure box from inside. Her treasure box was the only thing she had from when she was really little. She didn't know who had given it to her, but she liked to think that it was a present from her real mother. It was the sort of box a mother would give a little girl, because it had once been filled with cookies. She could still see faded pictures of them on the lid. Sometimes, if she tried hard enough, she could almost remember her mother giving it to her to keep her special things in. "Why don't you keep your things in here, darling?" her mother had asked. "Then they'll never get lost."

Margo kept her most prized possessions in her treasure box. There was the small pink rattle she'd had as a baby. There was a bracelet made of glass beads that she'd been given for her sixth birthday. There was a beautiful lavender silk ribbon that someone had let her have from a box of chocolates. And now there was Mrs. Smith's Victorian jewelry. Margo had found enough money in the safe to get herself a bus ticket to California. It was safer to pawn the jewels in California, she'd decided, where no one would be looking for her. Once Mrs. Smith realized they were gone—once they found that bloated little body—the police would be after her. She had to be as careful as she could. She smiled down at the sparkling jewels. Everything had gone just exactly as she'd planned. Exactly as her voice had told her it would.

The doors closed and the bus shook as the heavy engine started up.

Easy as pie, Margo thought as they slowly

pulled out of the bus station. *Like feeding cookies to a fat little brat.*

Margo gazed out the window as the bus pulled out of town. Her skin tingled. *We're on our way!* shouted her voice. *We're finally on our way!*

"California, here I come," said Margo softly as they left the darkness of the depot.

She couldn't hear Georgie anymore. At first, even when she was sure he was dead, she'd heard that gurgling sound he'd been making. She'd gone back to the blanket and collected the picnic things, and still she'd heard him splashing. She kept looking back at the lake, to see if he really were still kicking, to see if he was following her out—but no, he was floating there on the dirty water of the lake. Like a fat, dead duck. And now he was quiet.

"Poor little Georgie Porgie," said Margo with a happy smile. A rhyme from her childhood ran through her head. *Georgie Porgie, pudding and pie, kissed the girls and made them cry.* Margo started laughing. "Georgie Porgie, pudding and pie," she recited in a whisper. "Ate too many cookies and had to die."

Chapter 5

"What is this place?"

Nicholas, still shaky from the ride on the back of Jakki's Kawasaki, was staring at the windowless cement-block building with a mixture of curiosity and terror. The parking lot was filled with motorcycles, and the door was guarded by a very large man with a shaved head and a ring through his nose. A thunderous din that couldn't really be called music was coming from inside; outside, a crowd of boys with beer cans in their hands were shouting and shoving each other, pretending to start a fight. At least Nicholas hoped they were pretending.

Jakki, her attention on locking her bike, didn't even glance at him. "It's Club Mud," she said. "I can't believe you had to ask." She took off her helmet. "It's the best place around."

The best place for what? Nicholas wondered, but he was too busy staring at Jakki to speak. It looked like she hadn't made any effort at all for this date. As far as he could tell, she was wearing the exact same clothes she'd worn on *Hunks*. Now that she'd removed the helmet, however, he could see that he'd been wrong. She'd not only put a purple streak in her hair, she'd painted a small and very unattractive *lizard* in the middle of her forehead.

"Come on," she ordered, striding ahead of him. "Let's party!"

Club Mud was not Nicholas Morrow's idea of a party. It was small, dark, and crowded. It was so noisy he literally couldn't hear himself think. The guys in the band—at least he assumed they were the band, since they were onstage, screaming and banging their instruments—all looked as if they'd just gotten out of jail. Which at least made them fit in with the rest of the crowd.

Nicholas however, in his green slacks and blue T-shirt, fit in the way a clown would at a convention of undertakers. Everyone had stared at him as he followed Jakki in.

Jakki hadn't noticed. She'd been too busy punching people in the arm and being punched back, a ritual Nicholas decided must be similar to shaking hands.

"Get me a beer," she yelled at him when they finally reached the bar.

He felt like saying *I see you're conventional enough to let me pay, Miss Rule-Breaker,* but it took too much effort to try to make himself heard.

The bartender glared at him menacingly, which Nicholas took to be a request for his order.

"One beer and one mineral water," Nicholas shouted.

It was amazing, but in a place where you could have landed a helicopter without anyone hearing, everyone at the bar managed to hear him say "mineral water."

They all thought it was pretty funny.

"Mineral water!" the bartender roared. "What do you think this is, a health club?"

"Hey, Jak!" someone shouted across the bar. "Where'd you find Mr. Suburbs? He lost or something?"

"Nah," Jakki screamed back when she stopped laughing enough to speak. "He's getting a taste of real life."

So this is real life, Nicholas thought as several bikers who looked like they'd probably been in the same prison as the band shoved him deeper into his corner. From what he could deduce from the chains and studs and scars that most of the guys were covered with, real life was very closely linked to real death. Nicholas carefully took a sip from his glass of tap water, trying to find a clear spot on the rim, and surveyed the crowd.

He hadn't seen Jakki since she'd grabbed her beer. Every once in a while, he caught a glimpse of her, laughing and slapping her friends around, but as far as he could tell, she'd forgotten about him completely.

Nicholas checked his watch. He'd been here only half an hour, but it seemed like at least three days. If he waited for Jakki to take him home, he'd probably be here for what felt like the rest of his life.

Screaming "Excuse me!" Nicholas fought his way to the pay phone by the entrance, trying not to get dragged into the jumping and shoving that was Club Mud's idea of dancing.

Olivia answered on the third ring.

"You're *where?*" she shrieked. "Isn't that a biker hangout?"

"Olivia!" he shouted. "Olivia, this isn't funny. Just get in your car and come get me."

She tried to control her laughing. "But I'm watching a video, Nick," she spluttered. "I'm at the most dramatic moment. And I'm not dressed. And my hair's a mess. And—"

"Olivia!"

"I'm on my way."

Bruce had chosen a corner table, where he would be able to see Pamela come into the restaurant. That way he would be the one in control.

He sipped at his glass of ice water, his eyes on the door. *I am in control,* he told himself. *I know exactly what I'm going to do.*

He took another sip of water and tried to look at something other than the door.

He was going to listen politely to what Pamela had to say, and then he was going to tell her what *he* had to say! That it didn't change anything. He'd made up his mind about that. Whatever her excuse, he wasn't going to let himself get involved with her again. That was a firm decision. He would tell her that they'd been a mistake right from the start. He'd suffered enough when Regina died; he didn't want to suffer again. His eyes, controlled by some force other than his mind, darted toward the door. He knew Pamela could make him suffer. She had already proved that. He wasn't going to give her the chance to prove it again.

When Pamela appeared in the doorway of the Box Tree, Bruce realized how fickle and unreliable the human heart is. You told it how to behave, and then it went right ahead and did something else. He'd told his heart that it wasn't interested in Pamela anymore, and what happened? The minute he saw her, he fell in love with her all over again.

She looked beautiful. She had a red scarf wound through her black hair, and her eyes were shining like a blue sky after a rainy day. She looked like an angel. She looked like a girl any guy would give his right arm for, just to say hello to her. When she saw him, Pamela smiled. Bruce's heart took another leap, and his water glass crashed to the floor.

He was trying to pick up the pieces when she arrived at the table. "Let me help you," she said, immediately kneeling on the floor beside him.

"It's OK," he said quickly, trying not to look at her. This close, her perfume was making him feel dizzy. "I don't want you to cut yourself."

"And I don't want *you* to cut *yourself*. You're picking up that broken glass like it's paper."

"No, I'm not." He tried to move far enough away from her so that he could smell something besides her perfume, and whacked his head on the edge of the table.

"Oh, Bruce, are you all right?"

"Of course I'm all right. I—Ow!"

"Let me see that," she said, taking his hand.

101

He would have been fine if she hadn't touched him. If she hadn't touched him, he would have remained outwardly calm and in control, despite his inner turmoil. But suddenly all he could think of was how much he loved her. He got to his feet so quickly that he hit his head again.

"Maybe we'd better sit down," he said desperately. He collapsed in his chair as though it were a life raft.

She took the seat across from him. "It's good to see you," she said softly.

Bruce dove behind the menu. "Umph," he said.

"I'm really glad you agreed to meet me," said Pamela.

"The salmon's pretty good here," said Bruce, trying to regain his composure. He was afraid she would hear his heart, it was making such a racket.

She leaned across the table and took the menu from his hands. She touched him again. How could he have such strong and wonderful feelings for her if she was as bad as everyone said?

"Bruce," she said firmly. "I know this is hard for you, but it's hard for me, too. This whole last year at Big Mesa has been a nightmare for me. But I can free myself from it now, I know I can. If you'll just—"

"Well, well, what have we here? Bruce Patman and our own lovely Pamela."

Pamela's face went white, but she kept her eyes looking straight ahead, across the table. Bruce, however, turned to the three boys standing beside their table. He recognized them all. One was the guy he'd seen Pamela with, that awful morning in front of her house. The other two were on the Big Mesa football team, but they were much better at making trouble than they were at playing ball. *Big Mesa morons,* he thought. *If someone gave them a brain, they wouldn't know what to do with it.*

"What's the matter, Patman?" asked the one Bruce recognized as a linebacker. "You so desperate you have to scrape the bottom of our barrel now?"

They were looking for trouble, as usual, but he wasn't going to let them rile him. "What are you guys doing here?" he replied evenly. "Somebody leave your cage open?"

"Oh, ha ha ha," said the pimply one. "You think you're so cool, don't you, Patman? But if you were, what would you be doing with a piece of trash like this, huh?"

The third guy, the one who'd been with Pamela that morning, leaned toward Bruce, his smile a leer. "She being *real* nice to you, Patman?" He turned to Pamela, touching her scarf. "I hope you're being real nice to Bruce, Pammy. He's a big shot, you know."

"Leave me alone, Jake!" She shoved his hand away.

Bruce pushed back his chair. There was something about seeing that creep touch Pamela that made him want to hit him. *OK,* Bruce decided, *if these jokers want trouble, then I'm just the guy to give it to them.*

"Bruce!" Pamela made a move to stop him, but he was already on his feet.

"Maybe you'd like to continue this discussion outside," he said coolly, his eyes on Jake. "We wouldn't want to get your blood all over the tablecloth."

"Are you crazy?" Pamela's eyes were still shining, but now they were shining with fear. "There's three of them, Bruce, you can't take them on."

The Big Mesa boys laughed.

"Listen to your girlfriend," said Jake. "She's not worth fighting over." He winked. "Believe me, I know."

Suddenly Bruce went cold. He could hear everyone around him talking, but he couldn't make any sense out of it. He could feel the eyes of the other diners turning toward him. He had to get away. He had to get out of there. What was he doing, trying to fight three thugs like these because of Pamela? No matter what he felt for her, this was how it would always be. No matter what her defense was, this was what people thought of her. Was he going to spend the rest of his life fighting creeps in parking lots because of her? In a blind panic, he threw some money on the table.

"You liar!" Pamela slapped Jake so hard that the woman at the next table let out a horrified gasp. "You ugly, despicable liar!"

But Bruce was already halfway to the door, and he didn't turn around.

Steven came into the house through the back door, expecting to find the family in the kitchen, but the room was empty. He put his bag down and headed toward the living room.

"Hi, everybody," he called as he strode down the hall. "Guess who's home?"

He looked around in dismay. No one was there.

"Mom!" he shouted. "Dad!"

The house was silent. Well, what did he expect? It was Friday night. Most people went out on Friday night.

That made him feel a little better. Maybe things weren't so bad after all. If they were all out, maybe his father was telling the truth, and everything *was* almost normal. For the first time in days, Steven felt himself relax.

He hummed to himself while he fixed something to eat. Then he heard the front door opening, followed by his father's voice.

"It looks as though my son has come home unexpectedly," Ned Wakefield was saying in an apologetic voice, "but Elizabeth isn't back yet, I'm afraid. Something must have held her up."

Steven came out of the kitchen. His father was standing in the living room, with a tall, stocky man in an expensive-looking dark gray suit and silver-rimmed glasses. Mr. Wakefield looked anxious. The other man looked bored.

This must be the hot-shot lawyer, thought Steven.

"Steven, what a surprise!" His father was smiling at him, but Steven could tell from the look in his eyes that the surprise was not a pleasant one. "Let me introduce you to Alan Rose."

Mr. Rose extended his hand without any enthusiasm.

"My son, Steven," said Ned Wakefield. He put a hand on Steven's arm. "Mr. Rose is going to be handling Elizabeth's case," he explained. "He has one of the finest legal reputations in California when it comes to this sort of thing." He turned back to Alan Rose, patting Steven's arm. "Steven is in college now," he informed him. "He's going to make a fine lawyer himself someday."

Mr. Rose was as impressed by this news as he would have been to hear that Prince Albert had been given a bath the day before. "We'd better get started," he said, ignoring Steven completely. "Time is money, you know."

Ned Wakefield laughed uncomfortably. "Of course," he said as he directed Mr. Rose toward the living room. "Whatever you say."

Steven couldn't get over how nervous his father seemed. It wasn't like him at all. His father usually exuded confidence. Steven's feelings of calm and normalcy completely evaporated. He'd been right to come home. Things were obviously worse than he'd thought.

Mr. Rose opened his attaché case and started putting papers on the coffee table in front of the couch. "I wouldn't mind a cup of tea," he said as he took a gold pen out of his pocket and placed it on top of his notepad. He looked at his watch.

"Tea. Of course," said Mr. Wakefield quickly. "Steven, why don't you fix Mr. Rose a cup of tea?" He looked at his own watch. "I'm sure Elizabeth will be home any minute," he apologized. "She and my wife both knew what time you were coming."

Steven was happy enough to escape from the presence of Alan Rose. *What a creep,* he thought as he headed back to the kitchen. *No wonder Dad didn't want me around.*

Steven was just putting the tea on a tray when he heard his mother's car in the driveway. He stopped what he was doing and hurried to the back door.

He saw her before she saw him, and all his fears were confirmed. His beautiful sister looked ghastly. She was thinner than she'd ever been, and there were dark circles under her eyes. Just from her walk, slow and deliberate, looking at the ground, he could see the enormous strain she was under.

"Elizabeth!" he cried as she neared the house.

Elizabeth looked up in surprise. Then her expression turned to one of pure joy. As soon as she saw him smiling at her, she ran and threw herself into his arms.

"Oh, Steven," she said, her voice breaking. "I'm so glad you're home!"

He rested his cheek on her head. "I am too," he told her. "I am too."

"You know, Miss Wakefield," Alan Rose was saying in his grating, patronizing way, "if you don't cooperate, there isn't much I can do to help you."

"I *am* trying to cooperate," Elizabeth protested weakly. She closed her eyes, trying again to bring back that night. "I don't even remember driving," she said hopelessly. "All I remember is light in my eyes. And then the brakes squealed . . . and there was glass shattering . . . and . . . and someone was screaming but I don't know which of us it was."

Steven looked over at his parents, sitting side by side on the sofa. It was difficult to tell from their polite expressions what they were thinking. What had gotten into his father, letting a slick, insincere guy like this defend Elizabeth? Couldn't they see the condition the poor kid was in?

The lawyer leaned back in Ned Wakefield's leather armchair. "Miss Wakefield—Elizabeth . . . Let me explain this to you as clearly as I can. I am your lawyer, and if you tell the truth to no one else, you tell the truth to me, because I have to decide how best to defend you."

Steven shifted in his chair, about to say something, but he caught his father shaking his head at him, so he kept still.

Mr. Rose folded his hands on his lap. "Now, do you seriously expect me to believe that you don't remember *anything* that happened that night?"

Elizabeth nodded. "But I *don't* remember anything," she said, close to tears again. "I wish I did."

The lawyer sighed. "And what about this lab report?" he persisted. "There was alcohol in your blood, but you maintain that you weren't drunk."

Steven jumped to his feet. "My sister doesn't drink."

"There was alcohol in her blood," Mr. Rose repeated. "It didn't get there through osmosis, you know."

"But I *don't* drink," said Elizabeth. "I've never been drunk in my life."

Mr. Rose gave her a disgusted look. "You say you don't remember anything that happened that night," he reminded her. "So how do you know that you weren't drunk?"

"Now, see here!" This time it was Mr. Wakefield who interrupted. "I don't like what you're insinuating."

Mr. Rose opened his attache case and began to put his papers way. "I'm not insinuating anything," he said testily. "But if your daughter can't come up with more than this, then the best advice I can give you is to have her plead guilty. We should be able to get her a light sentence because she has no previous record and has always been a model student—maybe six months in a juvenile home."

Mrs. Wakefield caught her breath. "Oh, no!" she cried. "But I thought—"

Mr. Wakefield cut her off. "That's not good enough," he told the lawyer. "Elizabeth is innocent, and I want her acquitted."

Mr. Rose snapped the locks on his attaché case

shut. "Well, I'm afraid this is the best I can do."

Mr. Wakefield got to his feet. "Then I'll have to do it myself."

Alan Rose picked up his case. "Whatever you say," he said. He treated them all to his idea of a smile. "But I don't envy you your job." He looked at Mr. Wakefield. "It's going to be hard to convince a judge that Elizabeth is innocent when Elizabeth isn't even sure herself."

"Don't tell me!" Lila ordered as they stopped in the entrance to the Beverly Hills Hotel. "Let me see if I can pick her out."

Lila's father put his hand on her shoulder. "To tell you the truth, I'm not sure I'll recognize her myself," he confessed with a laugh. "It's been a very long time."

Lila's eyes impatiently scanned the room. Not the woman in blue. Not the redhead. Not the woman with the scarf. Not the woman wearing the wig. Not the—

"Grace." Her father's voice was almost a whisper.

Lila turned in the direction he was looking. "That's her, isn't it?" asked Lila, her eyes on the elegant woman sitting by herself at a corner table, idly looking through the menu. Except for her ash-blond hair and her porcelain skin, she looked so much like Lila that Lila was sure she would have recognized her even if they'd met on the street.

Mr. Fowler's hand tightened on his daughter's shoulder. "Yes, that's her."

Lila couldn't take her eyes off her mother. "She's beautiful."

Mr. Fowler gave her a gentle push forward. "Why don't we go over there and you can tell her so yourself."

"Isn't her boyfriend supposed to be with her?" Lila whispered as they made their way across the crowded restaurant. "Where do you think he is? Do you think this means we have her to ourselves?"

Mr. Fowler laughed. "Lila, I just got here too, remember? I have no idea where this Pierre character is."

Grace looked up at that moment, and her eyes went straight to Lila. Lila's heart skipped a beat. When her mother smiled it was like throwing back the curtains on a sunny summer morning.

"Lila! George!" Grace held out a slender hand to each of them, but it was Lila who had her attention. "I can't tell you how happy I am to be here," she said gently. "I really and truly am."

Lila couldn't speak. She was staring into her mother's soft gray eyes, a million thoughts in her head and a million emotions in her heart. She couldn't think of anything to say that wouldn't sound silly. She couldn't very well just say "Hi," could she? She couldn't even say "How was your flight?"

She turned to her father for help.

Her father was leaning against the table, grinning like someone in a toothpaste commercial. "Well . . ." he finally said. "Well, Grace . . ."

Grace laughed, squeezing Lila's hand. "Why don't you two sit down? You must be exhausted, driving all the way from Sweet Valley."

Lila more or less fell into the nearest chair.

"Well . . ." said her father again. "It's been a long time."

"Too long," said Grace, smiling at Lila. "Much too long."

Lila smiled back, but she still couldn't find the words to say what she was feeling: that she was so happy to see her mother, she wanted to cry. She slipped her hand into the pocket of her jacket, where she'd put the photograph she'd found of her and Grace, sitting on a sofa, smiling at the camera as though they would always be together. She'd spent a lot of the day imagining the moment when she showed it to her mother. Grace would remember when the picture was taken. *Oh, that was the day I bought you the cutest little teddy bear, she'd say. Or, that was the afternoon you first said "Mommy."*

There would be tears in both their eyes.

Showing just a hint of unease for the first time, Grace glanced over at Mr. Fowler, and then back to Lila. "I don't know what your father has told you about me," she began.

"N-nothing," answered Lila. "I mean—"

Grace reached across the table and put her hand on Lila's. "I want to tell you everything you want or need to know about me," she said softly. "Even why I left you. Why I haven't been in touch." She swallowed hard. "It won't be easy for me, but I want you and I to—"

But Lila didn't find out what her mother wanted them to do, because at that moment a loud, almost theatrical voice interrupted her. It was a voice out of a comedy set in France.

"Darling!" it crowed. "Darling, here you are, buried away in the corner. I told the waiter there must be a mistake—Ms. Rimaldi couldn't possible be at a corner table, it is like putting a Ming vase in the cupboard, but no, he insisted—and for a change the waiter was right!"

Lila and her father both turned to look at the owner of the voice.

"It is the Fowlers!" he declared. "I would know you anywhere. You are so American. So perfectly American." He thumped himself on the chest. "And I, I am Pierre Billot, Grace's lover."

Lila almost choked. She'd never heard anyone describe himself as anyone's lover before. Her father, startled, knocked a fork off the table, muttering under his breath. Lila kept her eyes on the Frenchman. She couldn't help staring. Pierre Billot was about the same age as her father, but where George Fowler was solid and rugged, Pierre was wispy and frail looking. He was wearing a pink suit and his longish dark hair was tied in a very small ponytail. He either had a dab of shaving cream on his earlobe or was wearing a small white pearl earring.

"And this must be the daughter!" he exclaimed, grabbing Lila by the shoulders and exuberantly kissing her on both cheeks. "You are beautiful. Beautiful like your mother."

Grace laughed. Was it Lila's imagination, or did she really sound a little embarrassed?

"Do sit down, Pierre," she ordered. "Give someone else a chance to talk." She leaned toward Lila. "You'll have to excuse Pierre," she said. "Travel makes him very excited."

Pierre had turned to Mr. Fowler and was extending his hand. "The ex-husband," he said with mock formality. "You will be happy to know that I have heard almost nothing about you, so I bear you no ill feelings." He made a little bow. "How do you do?"

"I think I could use a drink," George Fowler replied immediately. He glanced at his daughter.

Lila could see that she and her father were thinking exactly the same thing: now that Pierre had joined them, there would be no opportunity to talk about anything serious. Indeed, from the way Pierre was already babbling on about the poor service on the plane and the effect the California air had on his sinuses, Lila doubted that anyone else would have much opportunity to say anything. She thought about the photograph in her pocket. She knew she wouldn't be showing that to her mother tonight.

Margo felt the wheels of the bus turning beneath her. Every turn meant she was a little farther away from awful Ohio and a little closer to perfect California. *Soon,* the wheels seemed to be saying. *Soon, Margo, soon soon soon.* The lights of distant houses shone through the dark like welcome beacons.

Soon I'll live in a house like those, thought Margo. *A beautiful house with a palm tree on the lawn. I'll be just like the other girls in those houses. I'll have a real mother and father, and maybe even a sister. I'll have my own room. I'll paint my room orange. Orange like a pumpkin. And I'll have a fluffy green rug and a real dresser to keep my things in. I'll keep my treasure box in the bottom drawer. My mother will help me pick out curtains. "You can have any curtains you want, honey," she'll say. "You can have anything you want." I'll have my own phone, too. I'll sit on my bed and I'll talk to my friends all night on the phone. "Isn't Margo popular?" everyone will say. "Isn't she perfect?" My family will love me so much . . .*

Margo wrapped her worn raincoat around her and curled up in her seat, gazing sleepily out of the window.

It had been a long day. Stealing the jewelry . . . killing Georgie . . . starting her journey . . . Her eyes closed. *Which will they discover first? That the jewelry's missing? That Georgie's missing? That I'm gone too?*

A smile flickered across Margo's lips as she remembered the look on Georgie's face when he realized what was happening. *It isn't true that only the good die young,* she thought as she drifted into sleep. *It's the weak who die young . . . the very, very weak.*

Chapter 6

Thank God, Todd thought as the hero and the heroine fell into each other's arms. *It's almost over.* Now maybe he could go home.

Years from tonight, if anyone asked him if he'd ever seen the movie he'd just sat through, Todd would truthfully be able to say, "No." He'd been afraid to let himself enjoy the movie because of Jessica, sitting beside him as if she was carved out of ice. They were the only two people in the theater who hadn't laughed through most of the picture.

Todd stifled a sigh. Unable to get into the film, he'd found himself thinking of Elizabeth instead.

So what else is new? Todd wondered as he

stretched the leg that had gone to sleep. It was beginning to seem that he would probably spend the rest of his life thinking about Elizabeth. How could he ever stop, when his lips could still feel the smoothness of hers, and his heart could feel nothing but the lack of her love?

The credits began to roll up the screen. Todd stretched, rubbing his neck. His whole body ached from sitting rigid and twisted for so long. He glanced uneasily at Jessica. She'd kept leaning toward him during the movie, which had made him so uncomfortable that he kept edging farther and farther over in his seat. Once she'd even reached for his hand. Luckily he'd been holding the popcorn.

Todd turned to Jessica as the lights came on. "Maybe this wasn't such a good idea after all," he said gently.

Jessica shook her head. "Oh, no," she said. "no, I really liked it. I really did. It was very funny."

But when she looked over at him he couldn't help noticing that there were tears in her eyes.

What a jerk I am, Todd scolded himself. *How insensitive can I be? Here I am thinking about myself, as usual, and poor Jessica's probably having an even tougher time. I miss Elizabeth so much, but at least she's still alive. I can always hope that things might work out someday. I can still dream. But Jessica can't. Sam is dead, and nothing could ever change that.*

Impulsively, he reached out and took her hand. "Why don't I take you home now, Jess?" he asked. He'd never felt very close to Jessica before, but now he was feeling almost brotherly toward her.

Her fingers closed around his. "Home?" she asked. She almost sounded frightened. "Do we have to go home so soon?"

Todd couldn't hide his surprise. She'd seemed so miserable all evening that he assumed she'd be anxious to get home as soon as possible. "It's just that you look really tired," he said quickly. "I thought—"

"Tired?" Jessica's laugh was as sharp as a carving knife. "Tired?"

Her voice was suddenly so low that he had to lean closer to hear her. To his surprise, she smelled just like Elizabeth.

"Don't you understand, Todd?" Jessica was saying. "I don't do anything anymore. I can't think of anyone but Sam." Fresh tears filled her eyes. "This is the first time I've been out since—" She broke off, desperately rummaging through her purse for a tissue.

Still reeling from the aroma of Elizabeth's perfume, Todd disengaged his hand. "We'll do whatever you want," he said quickly. "Would you like to go for pizza? Or maybe to the Dairi Burger?"

Jessica shuddered. "Oh, no," she said, her golden hair swinging as she shook her head. "It's Friday night, Todd. Everybody will be there. I couldn't face a lot of people now." She looked up at him shyly as he got to his feet. "Maybe we could just take a walk along the beach? There's a place we used to go to—"

"Sure," Todd agreed. "We'll take a walk along the beach." He gazed down at her red-rimmed eyes. "The fresh air will do you good," he said.

Amy stopped abruptly. "Do you see what I see?" she asked, grabbing hold of Caroline's arm.

Caroline, who had been checking her hair in the window behind them, turned to look across the street. "It's Todd and Elizabeth," she said with disinterest, her attention going back to her reflection. "Big deal."

Amy pulled on her arm. "No, it's not," she said. "Will you stop looking at yourself for a second and pay attention?"

Caroline turned around again. "Well, I'll be . . ." she said, giving a low whistle. "You're right. That isn't Elizabeth. It's Jessica." She

121

whistled again. "They seem pretty cozy. She's even holding his arm."

A worried look came into Amy's eyes. "Don't you think that's a little odd?" she asked. "I mean, forgetting that Elizabeth and Todd have been together forever, Sam's only been dead a few weeks."

Caroline laughed. "Oh, come on. You don't think that there's anything in it, do you?" She almost sounded disappointed. As one of the biggest gossips in Sweet Valley, if not all of California, she considered herself something of an expert on what was worth noticing and what wasn't. "Those two are about as compatible as a mouse and a boa constrictor."

Amy nodded slowly, but the worried look was still in her eyes. "I wonder where Elizabeth is, though," she mused. "Why isn't Todd with her?"

"Elizabeth's gone into hiding," said Caroline. "And who can blame her? She would have felt humiliated to have an overdue library book. Can you imagine how she must feel about killing her sister's boyfriend?" She shrugged. "Anyway, I heard Liz and Todd had split up," she continued. "Things weren't so good between them before the Jungle Prom, but after the accident it all fell apart."

Amy watched Jessica lean her head against

Todd as they walked slowly up the street. "I don't like it," she said. "I have a really strong feeling that something's wrong."

Caroline laughed. "Oh, come on, Amy. Todd's just comforting her, that's all. You know what a Boy Scout he is."

"It's not Todd I'm worried about, it's Jessica." Amy sighed. "She's been so bright and bouncy lately—as though nothing had happened. It just isn't normal."

"Well, you know Jessica," drawled Caroline. "She's always been on the flighty side."

"Ummm," said Amy. "I guess that's true." But secretly she was wondering if she really knew Jessica at all.

"So then," Nicholas was saying, "while I'm waiting for Olivia, a guy wearing about sixteen earrings and a leather jacket with a skull and crossbones on the back comes up to me and asks me if I'm a narc!"

Enid wiped tears of laughter from her eyes. If anyone had told her a few hours ago that she'd soon be sitting in a front booth in the pizzeria, laughing so hard her sides ached, she would have told them they were crazy. She was so worried about Elizabeth that she hadn't wanted to go out tonight, but Hugh Grayson, her boyfriend, had convinced her to. Now she was glad that he had. Olivia had brought Nick here to recover from his date with the Queen of Darkness. They had asked Hugh and Enid to join them. Nicholas was being so funny about his evening that Enid found herself relaxing for the first time in days.

"I don't believe it," Enid gasped. "He asked you if you were a *narc*?"

"Well, he certainly couldn't have thought that you were an *undercover* cop," put in Olivia. She turned to Hugh and Enid. "Believe me, I had no trouble finding Nick when I got there." She grinned. "He was the only one there without a tattoo."

Hugh winked at Nicholas. "So, are you going to go through with the rest of these dates, or are you going to quit while you're ahead?"

Nicholas laughed. "I'm not so sure I'm ahead now," he said. "The motorcycle ride alone took about ten years off my life."

Olivia jabbed him in the arm. "Oh, don't be such a spoilsport," she ordered. "At least you're getting out instead of sitting at home by yourself."

Something caught Enid's eye outside the window, and she glanced over just in time to see Jessica, her arm through Todd's, strolling up the street. The pizza she was eating turned to sawdust in her mouth. "He's not the only one who's getting out," she said flatly.

"What's the matter, Enid?" asked Olivia, following her gaze.

Nicholas squinted through the glass. "Hey, that's not Elizabeth," he said.

"Well done, Watson," said Olivia. "What's your next announcement? That the world's not really flat?"

Hugh looked at Enid. "I guess this whole awful tragedy has really shaken things up," he said quietly.

Enid bit her lip. "Including Elizabeth," she said, surprised at how angry she suddenly felt. What was Jessica doing with Elizabeth's boyfriend? And where was Elizabeth? She was the one who should be walking down the street with her arm in Todd's. She was the one he should be showing some support to.

Olivia turned to Enid. "I was a little worried before, when Liz was refusing to take my calls," she said slowly. "But I sort of figured things were all right, because she had Jessica and Todd and you. Everyone knows how important the three of you have always been to her."

Enid absentmindedly pulled a piece of cheese off her pizza, her eyes still following Jessica and Todd as they disappeared up the block. "But she doesn't have me," said Enid. "She's so unhappy and ashamed that she's keeping me away."

"Well, it doesn't exactly look as if she has Todd and Jessica, either," commented Hugh.

"No," said Enid softly. "Todd and Jessica seem to have each other."

The whole evening had been a stupid idea. She'd hated the movie with its dumb jokes and its happy ending, and she'd hated the rest of the audience for laughing so hard. And now she was hating this moonlight walk with Todd. What had made her think being with Todd could ever make up for not having Sam?

Jessica glanced over at Todd as they walked slowly up the beach, several feet of sand and dead seaweed between them. He had his hands in his pockets and his eyes on the ground. He'd been preoccupied all night. He hadn't said much on their way to the movie or when they were driving out from town, and he wasn't talking at all now. Whatever he was thinking about was taking all his attention. But Jessica no longer really cared. There was only one thing she really cared about—and it was the one thing she couldn't have.

Jessica raised her head, brushing a few loose strands of hair from her eyes, and stared straight ahead of her. Several yards down the beach, she could see Sam. He was wearing a white T-shirt and cutoffs, the outfit he'd worn the last time they'd picnicked on the beach. He was teasing her. *Bet you can't catch me!* he was shouting. *The loser has to kiss the winner until their lips hurt!* In her heart, she was running after him, sand flying around her, the moonlight making a path that led straight into Sam's arms.

Todd cleared his throat, upsetting the still-ness of the night; interrupting her futile memories. "So," he said hesitantly, "this was where you and Sam used to come all the time."

Jessica nodded, her eyes still on the vision of Sam, running faster and faster away from her through the sand. She'd lied when she told Todd that she and Sam always came to this spot. The spot that she and Sam always went to was far-ther up the coast, sheltered by a small grove of trees. Sam had even carved their names on one tree. But there was no way she was going there with someone else. Jessica kicked an empty crab shell out of her path. There was no way she would ever go there again.

Todd came to a stop, looking not at her, but at the pale sliver of the moon. "I guess it must be really awful for you," he said at last, his voice gentle. "You must miss Sam a lot." He took a deep breath. "Sam was a really nice guy, Jessica. He was really special."

Everyone else—including her parents—were afraid to talk to her about Sam. She could see it in their eyes. *Let's not bring up his name,* their eyes said. *Let's pretend that he never existed.* She could hear it in the things they did say— *time heals all wounds . . . you just have to keep yourself busy. . . .*

Todd's unexpected mention of Sam took Jessica by such surprise that she was instantly flooded by the emotions she'd been trying so hard to control.

Todd reached out for her. "Jessica—Jess— I'm so sorry."

She'd thought she had no tears left, but she'd been wrong. Todd's words had released the floodgates on her heart. Sobbing uncontrollably, Jessica slipped from Todd's grasp and fell to the sand.

Todd knelt beside her and put his arm around her shoulder. "It's all right," he kept saying. "It's all right, Jess. Just let it out."

She clung to him.

"I do know how you feel," Todd whispered. "I really do. I miss Liz so much, I feel like I'm losing my mind."

Liz. It wasn't Jessica he was concerned about. It wasn't Jessica he felt bad about. He didn't understand Jessica at all, or what she was going through. He didn't care about Sam or what a special person he'd been. All Todd cared about was Elizabeth. All he cared about was the person who had killed Sam.

Jessica pressed herself closer to Todd. "I should have known you'd understand," she said between her sobs. "I've always thought you were sensitive."

Todd took her lightly in his arms. "It's all right, Jess," he whispered. "I'm here with you now."

She leaned against him. *Yes*, thought Jessica. *And here is where you're going to stay.*

Pamela's room looked as though a tornado had passed through it. The dress she'd worn to the Box Tree was thrown over a chair like an old rag. One shoe was near the door and the other was in a corner. Her stockings dangled from the doorknob. Her gypsy-red scarf hung out of the wastepaper basket next to her desk.

In the center of the storm's damage, huddled on the bed as though it were a life raft, was Pamela herself, her face buried in her pillow. She was crying so hard that her body was shaking and the pillow was wet with tears.

I'll stay in this room forever, Pamela was telling herself. *I'll never leave the house as long as I live.*

She could imagine the shrubs outside growing up to the roof, the ivy covering the windows. She imagined children, years and years from now, pointing to the house and asking their mothers about the woman who lived inside. Their mothers would answer, "I don't know, honey. Nobody has seen her for years."

Then at least she'd have some peace. At least she'd know that everybody had stopped talking about her, spreading their rumors and their hateful lies.

Bruce. Whether she opened her eyes or kept them closed, she could still see his face as Jake and the others taunted him.

"I've been a fool," she mumbled through her sobs. "I've been a stupid, stupid fool." She'd thought that the way she and Bruce seemed to feel about each other would change everything. That with him beside her she could rise above all the lies. But Bruce believed the lies. He'd rather believe a creep like Jake than listen to her. He'd never really cared for her at all.

And now things were going to be even worse. Fresh tears streamed down her face. Pamela had planned to tell Bruce her news over dinner, but of course they'd never gotten as far as dinner, so she'd never had a chance. She'd arranged to transfer from Big Mesa to Sweet Valley High to get away from her ruined reputation. She'd been so sure she could straighten things out with Bruce—she'd been so sure the news would make him happy. But it wasn't going to make him happy. Now she could see that. Bruce had never loved her, and after tonight her reputation would follow her wherever she went.

Pamela pounded the bed with her fists. *I'm never leaving this house,* she repeated to herself. *Never, never again.*

Steven put his arm around Elizabeth as she turned to open her bedroom door. "You're sure you're all right, Liz?" he asked gently. "That Alan Rose character didn't upset you too much, did he?"

Elizabeth forced herself to smile. "Oh, no. No, he didn't upset me," she lied. "I'm fine, Steven, really. I'm just tired."

Steven gave her a hug. "You're right," he said. "You must be exhausted. I know what an ordeal this is for you."

His arms around her felt so strong and comforting that Elizabeth wished she could just collapse in them.

Steven slowly pulled away. "I'll see you in the morning," he said. "You get some sleep."

Elizabeth nodded. "We'll talk then," she said. "Good night, Steven."

As soon as the door shut behind her, her tears started again. Talk in the morning? What could they possibly talk about? Visiting hours in jail?

Elizabeth flung herself across her bed. As miserable and confused as she'd been feeling, she realized now that she'd believed her father when he'd said that everything was going to be all right. That he'd get her the best lawyer in California, and he'd prove her innocence once and for all.

Elizabeth moaned out loud. Alan Rose, the best lawyer in California, had thought she was guilty. He thought she'd be lucky to spend six months in a juvenile home. If her own lawyer didn't believe her, then who would?

Why can't I remember anything? Elizabeth asked herself as the tears spilled onto her pillow. *If only I could remember something. Anything. Even if it's something against me. I just can't stand this nothingness anymore.*

"Oh, why can't I remember?" Elizabeth sobbed out loud. "Why?"

Margo was dreaming.

It was still dark, very, very dark, but the bus suddenly pulled over to the side of the road. "Margo!" the driver shouted. "Margo! This is your stop."

Margo picked up her battered case and made her way down the aisle. Everyone watched her. "Where are you going?" they wanted to know. "Is someone meeting you?"

A little boy sitting by himself reached out and grabbed her jacket. "Can I come too?" he asked.

Margo gave him a shove. "Leave me alone!" she hissed. "Leave me alone!"

The bus driver was smiling. "Margo's stop!" he kept saying. "Margo's stop! Time to get off!"

Margo paused at the door and turned back. "But it's so dark out," she said to the driver. "It's so dark, and there's nothing out there."

The driver's smile was frozen. "Margo's stop! Time to get off!"

The doors opened. Margo couldn't believe what she was seeing. There, right in front of the bus, was a beautiful split-level house. It was the kind of house she'd always wanted to live in. It had a lawn as smooth as velvet, and shrubs and flowers all around. Everything about it looked warm and friendly. No one in this house would ever be mean. No one in this house would give her anything but love.

"Margo's stop!" the driver said once more. "Time to get off. Your family's waiting!"

Margo rubbed her eyes. He was right. There, standing at the open door of the house, was her family. Her mother, her father, and her beautiful sister. They were all smiling and waving at her. "Hurry!" they were calling. "Hurry, Margo! We've been waiting for you!"

Margo started to hurry down the steps, but as she did, something caught her, pulling her back. It was the little boy.

"Wait for me!" he whined. "Wait for me!"

Margo tried to push him away, but he was too strong.

"You can't go without me!" he screeched.

"Hurry, Margo!" called her family. "We can't wait forever, you know."

Margo was kicking and hitting the little boy, but he wouldn't let go. The harder she hit him, the harder he held on, and the harder he hit back.

The door still open, the bus started to move again.

"Wait!" screamed Margo. "Wait! I want to get off!"

"Not without me!" the little boy shouted. "Not without me!"

The bus began to pick up speed. Margo was crying and crying, but the little boy wouldn't let go. He started to drag her back into the bus. "Let me off!" she wept. "Let me off! Let me off!"

"Sorry, Margo," said the driver. The doors thudded shut. "Too late."

Too late . . . too late . . . too late . . . Margo woke up with her head pressed against the window and the first light of morning in her eyes.

She could still see her house and her family in her mind, but when she looked out the window, all she saw was the highway stretching before her. Miles and miles of highway.

Margo snuggled into her jacket. *I'm going to find my home and my family,* she told herself, *and no whiny little brat, or anybody else, is going to stop me.*

Chapter 7

Saturday morning Elizabeth woke to the sound of the newspaper thudding against the front door. *I can't face anybody this morning,* she thought as soon as she realized she was awake. *I just can't.*

Elizabeth had had a bad night. After Steven left her, she'd cried for what seemed like hours, finally falling into a troubled sleep. She'd woken up several times, her heart pounding, frightened by nightmares she couldn't remember. Now she felt exactly as she had after her night in jail. She just wanted to hide somewhere and never come out.

Elizabeth slipped quietly from her bed. Maybe no one was up and she'd be able to sneak downstairs to get herself a glass of juice. Then she could lock herself in her room for the rest of the day. She knew that Steven would want to talk to her, but she just couldn't. There was nothing to say.

She hurriedly got into her clothes and glanced at herself as she passed the mirror. Her skin was pale and her eyes were heavy with dark shadows.

"Please let them still be asleep," she whispered as she opened her bedroom door. She crossed her fingers and tiptoed down the stairs.

By the time Elizabeth realized that her mother was up and in the kitchen it was too late to sneak back upstairs.

"Elizabeth!" her mother cried, turning to her with a big smile. "You're up bright and early this morning. Do you have something planned for today?"

Something planned for today? Elizabeth stared at her mother in disbelief. Her mother must have noticed that no one came by to see Elizabeth these days and she could see that Elizabeth rarely left the house anymore. What did she think she had planned? A visit to the Sweet Valley Police Department to turn herself in?

Elizabeth shook her head. "No," she said, going over to the refrigerator as quickly as she could.

"You certainly are looking very nice this morning," her mother said to her back. "That shade of blue is very becoming."

Elizabeth froze with her hand on the juice pitcher. How could her mother say she looked *nice?* She looked haunted; haunted and ill.

"Thanks," she mumbled. She put the pitcher on the counter and got out a glass.

"I thought I'd make some pancakes for breakfast, since the whole family's here for a change." Her mother tilted the bowl toward her. "Apple and cinnamon. That's your favorite, isn't it?"

Elizabeth concentrated on pouring her juice. In her heart, she knew that her mother was just trying to keep things going as normally as possible, but after the meeting with Alan Rose, Elizabeth wasn't sure she could pretend at all anymore.

"Honey, did you hear me? Apple and cinnamon is your favorite, isn't it?"

"I'm really not hungry, Mom," said Elizabeth quietly. "I think I'll just have this juice and a cup of coffee."

"Oh, but you have to eat," Alice Wakefield said in the same chirpy voice. "You have to keep up your strength, you know."

"For what?" Elizabeth snapped back, her control suddenly gone. "For when I go on trial?"

Mrs. Wakefield stood for a second, her hand

still on the spoon she was using to stir the batter. In the next second she had put the bowl on the counter and taken Elizabeth in her arms.

"Oh, honey," she whispered. "I know this is awful for you, but it'll be all right. Your father says it'll be all right, and I believe him." She hugged Elizabeth close. "We know you're innocent, honey, and that's what matters most."

Elizabeth tried to hold back the tears. "But I can't remember anything," she said in a choked voice. "If only I could remember something . . ."

"You will," her mother said reassuringly, "You will in time. You have to give yourself a chance."

A sound in the doorway made them both look up.

Jessica was standing there, staring at them with a stricken look on her face that vanished as soon as their eyes reached her. She smiled. "Oh, please," she said, turning to leave. "Don't let me interrupt this touching moment between a mother and her daughter."

Mrs. Wakefield stared after her as she stormed away. "I wish I knew what was going on in her head," she said, thinking out loud. "I really wish I knew."

Lila was awakened by a knock on the door of her hotel room. "Go away!" she called sleepily, pulling the covers over her head. "I didn't order anything."

"Lila! It isn't room service. It's me."

Lila sat up suddenly, staring at the door, wondering if she'd really heard what she thought she did.

"Lila! It's me. It's Grace."

My mother!

"Just a minute!" she shouted back. "I'll be right there."

Lila leaped out of bed and grabbed her robe as she raced to the mirror. She looked OK. She fluffed up her hair. Yes, she definitely did look OK. Not beautiful, maybe—it wasn't easy to look beautiful first thing in the morning—but she looked OK. If there were a fire right now, she wouldn't feel embarrassed in front of the firemen.

"Lila!" Her mother's voice was filled with concern. "Are you all right, darling?"

"Yes, M—Grace," she answered, flinging herself at the door and wrenching it open.

Grace looked beautiful. It might be the first thing in the morning for Lila, but for her mother it was obviously more like late afternoon.

Grace had a tray in her hands. "I thought you and I might have a little coffee together before breakfast," she said with a smile. "It's difficult to have any girl talk when there are men around." Her eyes moved to Lila's bare feet. "Oh, sweetheart!" she exclaimed. "Don't tell me I woke you up!"

Lila shook her head. "Oh, no, no, I was awake." She ushered her mother into the room. "I just wasn't up, that's all."

Grace laughed. "I don't blame you," she said as she set the tray down on the small table by the window. "It's Saturday. Most Saturday mornings I wouldn't hurry to get up if the biggest dress sale in the world was being held in my living room."

Lila felt a wave of affection wash over her. This was the woman she had started to meet last night before Pierre the Pill had joined them. The woman who was warm and intelligent, funny and kind.

Grace handed her a cup of coffee. "Come on," she said, taking her own cup. "Let's sit on the bed and chat." She gave another dazzling smile. "You and I have a lot to catch up on." She sat down, patting the space beside her. "Now, which of us should start first?"

"Oh, you start," Lila said immediately. She was so bowled over by her mother's presence that she wasn't sure she could speak. "I want to hear all about what it's like living in France. It must be incredibly exciting."

141

Lila sat beside her mother, so close that anyone would have thought sitting together like this was something they did every day. It took some effort for Lila to keep her coffee cup from rattling in its saucer.

Grace talked happily about her life in Paris—the stores she shopped at, the restaurants and cafés she frequented, the people she knew—while Lila listened as if in a trance. Her mother not only had dozens of amusing and colorful stories, she also seemed to know everybody who was worth knowing on the continent of Europe.

But while her mother talked, the same questions kept repeating themselves in Lila's mind. *How long is she staying? When will I see her again? Will she want me to go with her? Will she ever come back?*

There were several times when Lila almost got up enough courage to ask those questions out loud, but by the time the coffee was finished she realized that her mother's life really was in Paris. This was a visit, and nothing more. Her mother's every-fourteen-years visit. She could never ask Grace those questions. She was too terrified of what the answers might be.

Her mother put a hand on hers. "Now, what about you?" she asked gently. "What about your life?"

Lila felt tongue-tied. It was a little difficult to know where to start. Should she start with last week or the week before? With last month? With last year? Should she tell her mother how lonely it was with George Fowler away so much? She had no idea what her mother might want to know.

Lila shrugged. "Oh, you know," she said, feeling herself flush. "I just go to school and to parties and things like that. Sweet Valley isn't exactly Paris, you know."

Grace's smile became even warmer. "It isn't exactly not Paris, either," she said softly.

Lila looked at her in surprise.

Grace squeezed her hand. "Your father told me what happened to you," she confided. "About that boy . . . and the counselor . . ."

The tenderness and concern in her mother's voice nearly made Lila burst into tears. This was what she'd been wanting and needing. This was what she'd been missing: Her mother to talk to. Her mother to tell her everything was all right.

Lila opened her mouth to speak, but then the telephone rang.

Grace reached over to the nightstand and lifted the receiver. "Oh, Pierre!" she cried. "Of course I haven't forgotten about you . . . Yes, I know you're starving. . . . Yes, darling, of course

143

I realize your system's upset. . . . Yes, my love, I'll be right down."

When she'd hung up, Grace made a helpless face at Lila. "I'd better go. He's working himself up into a terrible state. We'll meet you and George in the dining room." She touched Lila's arm again. "We'll continue our talk later," she said. "I really do want to hear about what's happened."

Lila felt as though she'd been about to throw herself onto a soft mattress and instead had landed on a slab of concrete. Grace wasn't really interested in her. After fourteen years, the best she had to offer was a few minutes in a hotel room. A few minutes that ended as soon as Pierre the Pill started demanding attention.

"Don't worry about it," said Lila coldly. She stood up.

Grace stood up too. "What do you mean, 'Don't worry about it'? I'm your mother. I care about you. I want to know."

Lila could feel her entire body beginning to shake. Where had her mother been for so long if she cared about her so much? Why had she stayed away? Why hadn't she been there all the times Lila had needed her?

Lila's voice broke. "You haven't been my mother for the last fourteen years," she said loudly. "What makes you think I want you now?"

"But, darling," Grace began. "If you'll just wait a moment, I can explain—"

Darling! Did she call everyone darling? Even the daughter she'd abandoned?

"Don't bother!" yelled Lila as she ran to the bathroom so she wouldn't cry in front of Grace. "I don't want any explanations."

She slammed the door.

Todd had been playing basketball most of the day. He'd hoped that a lot of strenuous activity would take his mind off both Elizabeth and Jessica.

Ever since last night, when he'd inexplicably found himself with his arms around the twin sister of the girl he loved, Jessica's tears seeping through his shirt, he'd realized that somehow and in some way, he was headed for trouble.

It wasn't that he didn't care about Jessica, or that he wasn't sympathetic to the awful ordeal she was going through. But something inside him was trying to warn him to keep his distance.

And that was the other reason he'd wanted to stay out of the house. Jessica had already called him twice that morning. The first time he'd pretended that the doorbell was ringing to extricate himself before she could ask him when she was going to see him again.

The second time he'd been smarter; he'd let

the answering machine take the call. "Todd?" Jessica's voice, soft and sad, had drifted across the living room. She'd sounded so unhappy that it was all he could do to keep himself from picking it up. "Todd? Are you there? It's me, Jessica. It's nothing important . . . I just need someone to talk to."

Now, as Todd came into the kitchen, the telephone was ringing again. Should he risk it? He looked at the clock. It was after four. It had to be safe. Jessica would be at the mall on a Saturday afternoon, up to her eyelashes in shopping bags. Todd reached for the phone.

"Oh, thank God it's you," Jessica said immediately. She sounded as though she'd been crying. "I've been trying to get you all day."

Todd shifted on his feet. It was amazing how guilty she managed to make him feel with so little effort. "I—I've been out," he stammered. "I promised Scott Trost I'd—"

"I've been having such an awful day," Jessica went on, uninterested in what Todd had promised Scott. "Saturday was the day I always went to watch Sam race—" Overwhelmed with emotion, she broke off.

Todd could feel his heart softening. How mean-spirited he'd been not to answer the phone earlier. How selfish.

"Oh, Jessica, I'm so sorry," he said sincerely.

146

"Why didn't I think? Of course, this must be one of the hardest days of all for you."

Jessica sniffled back some tears. "I guess I just have to get used to it," she said in little more than a whisper. "I just wish everyone else hadn't gone out today. My dad's working, my mom went shopping, and Steven took Elizabeth out—" Her voice caught again. "But I guess they didn't want me to go with them."

There was a second when Todd was standing there, looking at the clock, thinking about the plans he'd made to go over to Scott's for a game of chess later and how he'd been looking forward to it, and then that second passed.

Todd heard himself saying, "I'll tell you what, Jess. Why don't you meet me in town and we'll go for a walk or something?"

"Oh no," she quickly answered. "I'm sure you're busy, Todd. It's Saturday. You must have plans."

"Nothing that can't be changed," said Todd.

"That dumb dog!" Steven Wakefield jumped to his feet.

Prince Albert had been chasing a squirrel across the park until the squirrel raced up the nearest tree. Prince Albert, temporarily forgetting that he was a large dog and not a small squirrel, had followed. Now, suddenly realizing his mistake, he'd come to a stop, clinging to the trunk even as he was slipping back down.

Elizabeth was still laughing when Steven and the dog came back to the bench.

"It's nice to see you laughing," Steven said as he sat down beside her. "I was beginning to think it was a sight I might never see again."

"You're not the only one," said Elizabeth. "But you probably should take a picture, since I don't know when it'll happen again."

Steven put his arm along the back of the bench, turning toward her. "There's something I have to say to you, Liz."

He sounded so serious that he suddenly reminded Elizabeth of their father.

"I don't think any of us are ever going to get over Sam's death," Steven began slowly. "You don't get over something like that; you just learn to live with it. And I know that will take a lot of time for you, and there's nothing anyone can do about that." His voice became determined. "But there is something we can do about proving your innocence." He winked. "Especially now that dad's fired that Rose guy and agreed to let me help him."

For the first time since the nightmare began, Elizabeth began to feel a little less alone. Just for an instant something like hope flashed through her heart. But then reality returned. When she turned to him, her face was full of doubt.

"But, Steven, I *don't remember a thing*. Don't you think that's strange? Don't you think that maybe my mind is blocking it out because it knows that I'm guilty?"

Her brother shook his head. "No," he said flatly. "I don't think you're blocking it out because you know you're guilty. It's the most normal thing in the world for a person to lose all their memory of a traumatic event. And besides, what about the police's contention that you were drunk? No one at the dance saw you drinking anything but punch, and yet both you and Sam had alcohol in your blood."

"If only something—some little thing would come back to me."

Steven took her by the shoulder. "I think some little thing has come back to you, Liz."

"What are you talking about?"

Steven grinned, unable to hide his excitement. "Remember last night when you were talking to Rose?"

Elizabeth nodded, wondering what could possibly have her brother so excited. She had told Alan Rose the same thing she'd told the police. Nothing.

"Well, you said that you remembered light in your eyes and squealing brakes and the shattering windows."

Elizabeth nodded again. "That's right," she said. "That's all I remember. Nothing."

Steven gave her a shake. "But don't you see, Liz? It isn't nothing. It could be everything."

"I don't understand what—"

"The light, Liz! You saw light in your eyes! That's what you said. Well, if you saw light in your eyes, maybe it was because another car was coming toward you!"

Elizabeth frowned. She was sure she hadn't told the police about the light, but she did remember mentioning it last night. Where had that come from? She buried her face in her hands, trying to concentrate. That one awful moment, suspended in time, came back to her. She couldn't see him, but she knew that Sam was beside her. He was saying something. In front of her was a shadowy blackness. And then—out of nowhere—a sudden burst of light.

She raised her face to her brother's. "There was a light, Steven," she said slowly. "I'm sure there was." The look of unsureness returned. "But what if it was my imagination or something? What if it wasn't a car after all?"

Steven got to his feet, pulling her up after him. "But what if it was?"

Prince Albert loped ahead of Elizabeth and Steven as they walked back to the car.

"There's one other thing I've been meaning

to talk to you about," Steven said, glancing over at her. "And that's Jessica."

"Jessica?"

Just the mention of her sister's name was like a knife through Elizabeth's heart. She'd been trying for days to make Jessica talk to her—or at least listen to her—but no matter how hard she tried or what she said, Jessica still refused to have anything to do with her.

Steven nodded. "Yes, Jessica. I have the distinct feeling that she's been avoiding me since I've been home."

"She's avoided me ever since the accident," said Elizabeth, unable to hide the hurt in her voice. "She won't even look at me if she can help it."

Steven shook his head. "Dad said he thought Jessica was handling things pretty well. She's gone back to school, and she seems to be going out with her friends . . . But maybe he's wrong. Maybe she's taking it harder than he thinks. People show their grief in different ways."

Elizabeth pictured Jessica sitting with her friends in the cafeteria, laughing and chatting, and eyeing the boys just like she always did. It certainly wasn't the traditional way of showing grief.

"I know Mom's worried too, Steven, but I really don't know what to think." Elizabeth's voice broke with emotion. "All I know is that Jessica hates me. I miss her so much, but I don't think she'll ever forgive me for Sam's death." She laughed bitterly. "Not that I'll ever forgive myself, either."

Steven slipped his arm around her shoulder. "Maybe she just needs time," he said. "You know she always winds up turning to her family when things are bad, but maybe this is something she just has to deal with by herself."

Elizabeth, looking up to see where Prince Albert was, saw something that made her come to a sudden stop instead. Just coming over the hill in front of her, holding hands, their heads bent together in conversation, were Jessica and Todd.

"She seems to have found someone to turn to," said Elizabeth as the most bitter tears yet filled her eyes.

Saturday night Nicholas stood outside the front door of his second date, Susan Jax, giving himself a silent pep talk.

You can't always go by first impressions, he was telling himself. *Maybe she was just nervous in front of the cameras. She can't possibly giggle like that all the time. She wasn't really all that bad, if you're honest with yourself. She can't be as bad as Jakki, that's for sure. At least she looked like she goes out in daylight.*

Nicholas straightened his tie and dusted some fluff from the sleeve of his jacket. He blew a fly away from the flowers he'd brought. He'd had the florist put together an especially lavish bouquet, in the hope that if he acted as though this was going to turn out to be the date of his dreams, it would. *If you expect the worst, you're going to get the worst,* he warned himself. *Think positive! Expect the best and the best is what you'll get!* He rang the bell.

It took Susan so long to open the door that Nicholas, thinking the bell might not be working, was just starting to walk around the side of the house to see if there was another entrance.

"Hello?" she called, following that with a spurt of giggles. "Did you want something?"

Nicholas spun around. Susan was dressed in old jeans and a sweatshirt that said 'Laugh and the World Laughs With You.' No wonder she was asking him what he wanted. It didn't look as though she'd been expecting him at all.

"Hi," he said with a grin, holding the bouquet out as he strode back to the front door. "Remember me?"

Susan giggled.

Think positive, Nicholas reminded himself. *Maybe she's just a little shy.*

He tried again. "I'm Nicholas. Nicholas

153

Morrow? From the *Hunks* show?"

Susan giggled. "Of course I remember you," she said between titters. "You like water-skiing." The fact that he liked water-skiing not only seemed to be the only thing she remembered about him, it seemed to strike her as incredibly funny.

He smiled bravely, thrusting the flowers into her hands. "That's right. I like water-skiing. And you like musical comedies."

He figured he must have remembered correctly because she started to giggle again.

"So." Nicholas rocked back and forth, waiting for her to invite him in.

Susan giggled into the flowers.

He made a show of looking at his watch. "I booked a table for eight thirty," he said. He cleared his throat. "Maybe you should get dressed," he suggested. "So we're not late."

Susan started giggling again. "Don't be silly," she said. "I *am* dressed."

By the time they were seated at their table—not at the expensive French restaurant he had planned on, but at Bobo's Burger Barn, the only place that would allow Susan in in her flip-flops—Nicholas had figured out how the dating world worked. If you expected the worst, you got the worst. If you expected the best, you got the worst.

"Look at this, isn't it neat?" Susan was saying.

Nicholas, trying to duck out of the reach of the giant spider plant that was attacking him, looked over at her. Not surprisingly, she was giggling.

She was also holding up a jelly glass filled with fat crayons. "See? You can draw on the tablecloth!" Illustrating what she meant, she began to draw a large smiley face on the paper tablecloth with a red crayon.

Nicholas watched, fascinated. How could someone hold a crayon steady while laughing like that?

She looked up, giggling triumphantly. "Isn't it neat?" she demanded.

Nicholas forced his mouth into a smile. "It's neat," he agreed. "It's very neat."

If she didn't stop giggling soon, he wasn't going to be responsible for his actions. He looked at the crayons in the glass, wondering what would happen if he stuffed them in her mouth. Would it make her shut up, or would it only make her laugh more?

His thoughts were interrupted by a new bout of giggles. "And you know what else?" she was asking him. "This isn't even the best part."

Somehow, in the confines of the tiny restaurant, her laugh was even more annoying than it was in the television studio, or outdoors, or even in his car. It sounded like the laugh of the killer doll in a cheap horror movie.

"Really? You mean it gets better?" Nicholas clutched his water glass, trying to ignore the fact that several other diners were darting glances in their direction. Maybe if he were lucky, one of them would stuff the crayons in her mouth for him.

She nodded vigorously, a gesture that produced even more merriment. "When you leave, they give you a balloon."

"A balloon, huh?" They'd better give him more than a balloon. They'd better give him a tranquilizer or he'd never make it home.

Susan nodded and picked up the glass of soda the waiter had put in front of her.

My God, this is it! thought Nicholas as Susan sipped her drink and quiet descended. *If I just keep her eating and drinking, it'll be all right!*

But the silence didn't last. Almost immediately the giggling started again.

"Ooh," said Susan. "The bubbles tickle my nose."

Boy, would I like to tickle your nose, he thought. But out loud he said, "So you've been here before, Susan?"

"Oh, sure," said Susan. "I come here with my boyfriend all the time."

For perhaps an entire second, he thought he

hadn't heard her right. Had she said that she came here with her *boyfriend*? He stared at Susan, who giggled as the waiter set her chicken burger and french fries in front of her. She had a *boyfriend*? Who? Chuckles the Clown?

"My boyfriend likes the chili," she informed him.

Nicholas was sure that it had to be some sort of Guinness record that she could talk, eat, and laugh all at the same time.

At last he felt capable of speaking. "Your boyfriend?"

She shook her head, giggling at how slow the ketchup was coming of the bottle. "My boyfriend once had a food fight here with the chili. It was really funny."

"You have a boyfriend?"

She beamed at him across the table. "Uh-huh. His name is Tampa. He's really neat."

"Susan . . ."

"What?"

Nicholas pushed his plate away, leaning forward so that she couldn't miss one word of what he was saying.

"Susan, why did you go on *Hunks* if you already have a boyfriend?"

She smiled back at him as though he'd asked why she put a coat on when it was cold. "Oh, you know. I just did it for fun."

"Oh, right," said Nicholas. "So this is fun. I was wondering what it was."

Margo sat behind her cheap dark glasses, watching the other passengers come back to the bus. She didn't get off the bus anymore unless it was to change to a different one. Not since the news about Georgie had started appearing on the front page of every daily paper in the country. Since then, Margo kept on her scarf and her sunglasses and changed her route as often as she could.

The woman who was sitting in front of Margo came back up the aisle. "Here's your paper, dear," she said. "And two chocolate bars and a cheese sandwich."

Margo had counted out the money for the candy and the paper to the penny. She'd figured out exactly how much money she could spend if she was going to have enough to get her to Albuquerque, and the amount she could spend got her two candy bars and a newspaper in the afternoon, and a soda and bag of chips at night. Albuquerque seemed far enough away from Ohio to be safe.

She pushed the sandwich back. "I didn't ask for a sandwich."

The woman shoved it into her hand. "Oh, I know, dear, but they were the last they had, so they gave me two for the price of one."

Margo looked at the sandwich. When she finally got home, her real mother would make her as many sandwiches as she wanted. Real sandwiches on thick bread with butter and mustard and those tiny green pickles Margo remembered having one Christmas. Her stomach growled. She didn't need to take charity. She could wait. She could wait until she got home.

"I don't want it," she snapped, practically throwing the sandwich back. "I'll be home soon. My mother will have a big dinner waiting for me."

"But you still have a ways to go," said the woman, holding the plastic container toward her. "I'm sure a cheese sandwich won't spoil your appetite."

"My mother is very careful about what I eat," said Margo. "She makes everything herself."

The woman sat down. "There aren't many who do that nowadays," she said over the back of her seat. "You're a very lucky girl."

Margo stared down at her lap, and at the photograph of Georgie smiling up at her from the newspaper. *Boy Found in Lake,* said the caption. "It's because of my brother," Margo said. "My baby brother. He died very young because of something he ate."

The woman turned around sharply. "Oh, my

dear, I'm so sorry. I hope he didn't suffer much."

Margo shook her head. "Oh, no," she said, remembering Georgie's face as the last breath left his body. The expression on his lips had been almost a smile. "He hardly suffered at all."

Chapter 8

Jessica lay on her bed, the sheet pulled over her face, listening to the rest of the family having Sunday breakfast out by the pool, the way they sometimes used to when Steven still lived at home. On those occasions, her father would go to the bakery for fresh rolls, her mother would squeeze fresh oranges for juice, Steven would fry the bacon, and she and Elizabeth would take turns making the main dish: a potato omelette if it was Elizabeth's turn; scrambled eggs with cheese if it was hers.

Jessica closed her eyes against the sunshine that was trying to make its way through the sheet.

Those days seemed like another lifetime.

The girl who used to make the scrambled eggs with cheese and chives no longer existed.

"Jessica!" she could hear her mother calling her from the yard. "Jessica! Why don't you come down and join us? Your brother will be leaving soon!"

Let him leave, Jessica thought angrily. Steven wasn't worried about her. Elizabeth was the reason he'd come home suddenly, not Jessica. Even though Elizabeth was fine. Elizabeth wasn't even going to jail, according to what Jessica had heard her father say. The worst that was going to happen to Elizabeth was that she might have to go to a juvenile home for a few months. That was all. A few months someplace in the country, where everyone would probably feel sorry for her, and then she'd come back and everybody would act as though nothing had happened.

Elizabeth would be queen of the world again. But Sam would still lie buried in the Bridgewater cemetery. And Jessica would still have a broken heart.

"Jessica!" It was Steven's voice. "Jess, please come down. Dad got some of those chocolate pastries you like so much."

Jessica laughed. It was funny, really. Your whole world collapses around you and everyone thinks all they have to do is buy you a chocolate pastry to make it all right again.

"What about me?" Jessica whispered. "Steven feels sorry for Liz, but what about me? I'm the one whose boyfriend is dead."

"Jessica?" Steven's voice was coming from the other side of her door. "Jessica, let me in. I want to talk to you."

"I told you. I don't feel well," she called back. "Go away."

"You've been avoiding me all weekend, Jess. I can't leave without at least saying good-bye in person."

Jessica pulled the sheet from her face. "Good-bye!"

"Jess—please . . ."

At least her room looks the same, Steven thought with relief as his sister opened the door. There were piles of clothes and books on every surface, including the floor. It was a amazing that she could even get into the bed, there was so much stuff on it.

"I'm really sorry I didn't come down, Steven," Jessica said as she threw herself into her armchair. "But I have a splitting headache." She grinned at him. Another thing that hadn't changed. "I feel like the whole Sweet Valley cheerleading team is dancing in my head."

Steven began to relax a little. Maybe Jessica really hadn't come down to breakfast because she wasn't feeling well. Maybe it had nothing to do with avoiding him or Elizabeth.

He made a little room for himself on the foot of her bed. "Is that why you've been staying away from me since I got here? Because you've had the Sweet Valley squad jumping around in your head?"

Jessica laughed. Her laugh always reminded him of a sunny day.

"I haven't been staying away from you, Steven. It's just that I've been so busy." She tossed her golden hair. "And you've been pretty busy too."

Here was something else that hadn't changed. Jessica could still be jealous of Elizabeth. "You know Elizabeth wasn't the only reason I came down. I'm worried about you, too."

Jessica snuggled a little deeper into her robe. Her big blue-green eyes widened. "Worried? About me? Why should you be worried about me?"

It was impossible to tell from the baffled expression on her face whether she was acting or not.

She gave him one of her biggest smiles. "You don't have to worry about me, Steven. I'm fine. I really am. My friends have been great; they've really rallied around me. And of course there's so much to do at school. . . ."

It was on the tip of his tongue to ask her if going out with Todd Wilkins was one of the many things she had to do at school, but he decided against it. Steven had come up here to try to get Jessica to talk to him, not alienate her completely.

He leaned forward and took her hand. "Jessica, I know what a difficult time this must be for you, but I want you to know that I'm here for you if you need my help. Anytime."

Jessica nodded. "I know that, Steven," she said. "But I don't need any help, I really don't." She smiled. "I'm really fine."

He looked into her blue-green eyes, but all he could see was himself, very small.

Todd couldn't imagine how it had happened. He'd been spending a quiet Sunday watching a game on television, the doorbell had rung, he'd gotten up to answer it . . . and now here he was, standing in the doorway with Jessica Wakefield in his arms.

"Jessica, what's happened?" he asked the top of her head. "What's wrong?"

But she was crying too much even to form a coherent sentence.

Thinking he saw a familiar car pass by, Todd started to draw her into the house.

"Come on in," he coaxed. "Sit down in the

living room. I'll get you something cold to drink."

But she wouldn't let go of him. She was clinging to him like moss to a rock. "Don't leave me," she sobbed. "I'm so alone, Todd. Please don't leave me."

He pried her hands from his shirt. "I'm not leaving you. I'm just going to get you something to drink." He pushed her gently onto the sofa. "And some Kleenex," he added, noticing her tear-streaked face. "I'll be right back."

Todd hurried into the kitchen, torn between concern for Jessica and concern for himself. It was bad enough that they'd practically walked into Elizabeth and Steven yesterday in the park. Without trying, he could still see Elizabeth staring at him, as cold and distant as the moon. He'd almost gone over to her right then, but Jessica had started crying again and he couldn't get away. At least she'd promised to explain to Elizabeth when she got home that it wasn't the way it might have looked; that they'd just been talking about Sam.

What worried him now was that he was positive that the car he'd seen pass the house was Lila Fowler's. There weren't that many lime-green Triumphs in California, and certainly not in Sweet Valley. If Lila had recognized Jessica, the news that he'd been standing in broad daylight with his arms around the wrong twin would be spread through Sweet Valley High like a brush-fire. Todd felt like sobbing himself. If that happened, he'd have lost any chance he had, no matter how tiny, of ever getting Elizabeth back.

When Todd returned to the living room, Jessica was lying on the couch with her face buried in a cushion. She looked so small and vulnerable—and so much like Liz—that he had to stop himself from taking her in his arms again.

Todd put the glass of water he'd brought on the coffee table and sat on the edge of the couch.

"Jessica," he said gently, passing her the tissues. "Jessica, please tell me what's wrong."

The golden head shook.

"Please, Jess. I can't help you if I don't know what's upset you like this."

She slowly pulled herself to a sitting position, dabbing at her eyes. "I—I—I can't," she stammered. "You'll think I'm being stupid."

He brushed a strand of hair out of her eyes. "No, I won't."

She twisted the tissue in her hands. "It's—it's Steven," she snuffled. "He's gone back to college and he never even talked to me about Sam. He didn't come near me all weekend." She moved closer. "I know he's worried about Elizabeth—

we're all worried about Elizabeth, even though we know she's innocent. But he could have saved a little of his sympathy for me. I'm going through a bad time too."

Somehow, Todd's arms found their way around Jessica again, almost as though they had a will of their own. "I know you are, Jessica," he comforted her. "I know you are."

She turned into his embrace. "I don't know what I'd do without you, Todd," she sighed. "I really don't know what I'd do."

Amy, staggering slightly under a load of brightly colored bags, followed Lila through the doors of the Sweet Valley Mall.

Lila, her own arms filled with shopping, lead Amy across the parking lot like a general leading her troops across a battlefield.

"When are you going to tell me?" gasped Amy when they finally reached the Triumph.

Lila dumped her packages in the back. "Tell you what?"

"Tell me what went wrong with your mother," said Amy, gratefully letting Lila take the packages from her arms.

Lila's smile was like a blank billboard. "What makes you think something went wrong?"

Amy's eyes went from Lila to the pile of purchases and back again. "Oh, let's just say it's a wild guess."

"Well, it's the wrong wild guess." Lila got into the driver's seat and slammed the door.

"Oh, come on, Li." Amy climbed in beside her. "All you talked about for days was Grace and what you were going to do together, and then you come back early and your only comment about the weekend is that you don't like her boyfriend."

Lila gunned the engine so hard that the Triumph almost jumped. "But I *don't* like him, Amy. He's a jerk."

Amy fastened her seat belt as they pulled out of the parking space.

"And what about all these things you just bought?" she demanded. Of all the bags Amy had been carrying, the only one that actually belonged to Amy was a small one containing a bottle of shampoo and a tube of conditioner. "Are you telling me that you went out and bought three pairs of cycling shorts—when you haven't been on a bike since you were six—because you don't like Pierre?"

A smile flickered at the corners of Lila's mouth. "No," she said, turning into the main road. "I bought the *bathing suit* because I don't like Pierre."

Amy leaned back in her seat. "Then why

did you buy the cycling shorts?"

"Because I had a fight with Grace."

Amy listened while Lila slowly and haltingly told her what had happened in L.A. When she was through, Amy looked over at her with a worried expression.

"Maybe you were a little hard on her," she said soothingly. "It can't be easy for her, suddenly meeting you after all these years. Imagine how guilty she must feel."

Lila made a sour face. "The only thing she seemed guilty about was leaving Pierre the Pill alone for a few minutes."

"Oh, come on, Li," said Amy. "You can't expect to make up for fourteen years in one weekend."

Lila made a sharp turn. "Yes, I can."

Amy was about to argue when something on the right caught her eye. "My God!" she cried. "I can't believe what I just saw."

"What?" asked Lila, her eyes on the road.

Amy looked behind them. "Todd Wilkins and Jessica in a clinch on his doorstep."

Lila laughed. "You're crazy. You'd catch Jessica in a clinch with King Kong before you'd catch her with Todd. It must have been Elizabeth."

Amy shook her head. "It wasn't, Lila. I'm sure it was Jessica."

"You're wrong. It had to be Elizabeth. Jessica thinks Todd's more boring than tofu."

"But Jessica's going through a lot of grief at the moment," Amy said thoughtfully. "Grief can make people do strange things."

"Not *that* strange," said Lila.

Amy was about to argue about it, when something to their left caught her attention this time.

"Well, if that was Elizabeth with Todd," she said, doing a double take, "who just passed us in the car with Enid?"

"With Enid?" Lila finally sounded doubtful.

"That's right, with Enid."

Lila glanced at Amy out of the corner of her eye. "I guess it's easier to accept the idea of Jessica with Todd than the idea of Jessica with Enid," she reluctantly admitted. "At least Jessica and Todd have been seen *speaking* to each other now and then."

"Yeah," said Amy, the image of Jessica standing within Todd's arms still in her mind. "It sure is easier."

Elizabeth stared out the passenger window while Enid drove, keeping up a steady stream of conversation about school and their friends. It had taken some persuading on Enid's part to convince Elizabeth to come out this afternoon, but now Elizabeth was glad she'd finally given in. Driving down the familiar streets, past the familiar sights, with her best friend describing an argument in the lunchroom, it was almost possible for Elizabeth to believe that things might someday go back to normal. That maybe Steven was right and she would be proven innocent. That people would forgive her, if not forget. That Jessica would stop hating her and love her again.

"Why don't we stop for a soda at the Dairi Burger?" Enid asked suddenly. "You look so pale; you could use a milk shake and an order of fries."

Elizabeth looked over. "I'd rather not, if you don't mind," she said slowly. "I'm really glad you suggested getting together this afternoon, Enid. It's making me feel almost human. But I really couldn't face all the kids at the Dairi Burger. Not yet. They'd all be looking at me and wondering when I'm going back to jail."

Enid bit her lip. "I understand how you feel, Liz. I really do." They came to a traffic light, and Enid looked over at Elizabeth, her eyes clouded with concern. "But I don't think half as many people are judging you as you think. Most of the kids I've talked to know it was just a horrible accident, and they feel bad for what you're going through."

Elizabeth turned back toward the window as the car moved forward again. "Jessica's judging me," she said in a hoarse whisper. "Jessica thinks I belong in jail."

Enid sighed. "Liz, listen to me," she said earnestly. "I know you and Jessica usually come together in times of trouble. But remember what you were saying about feeling so isolated and alone since the accident?"

Elizabeth nodded, but only part of her was listening to what Enid was saying. She'd just realized what street Enid had turned down. The street where Todd lived.

I can do this, thought Elizabeth. *It's just an ordinary street and an ordinary house. I can pass his house without closing my eyes or bursting into tears. I know I can. It's no big deal.*

"Well, just imagine how isolated and alone Jessica must feel," Enid was saying as they approached the Wilkins's home. "In some ways it might even be worse—" Enid broke off in horror as she realized where they were. "Oh, my God!" she gasped. "Liz, I wasn't paying attention. I had no idea—"

Elizabeth had been right. It was an ordinary house on an ordinary street. And parked in front of it was an ordinary Jeep. An ordinary Jeep that was usually parked on Calico Drive. Elizabeth felt so cold all of a sudden that it was as if the blood had been drained from her body and ice water put in its place. It was still hard to believe that it was the same Jeep she had wrecked: after its repair, it looked as good as new. If only the rest of her life could have been repaired so easily.

"I can imagine how alone Jess feels now," whispered Elizabeth, fighting back the tears. "I really can."

"Oh, Liz . . ." Enid's voice was almost a moan. "I'm sure it's not what you're thinking. I'm sure Todd's just being a sympathetic friend. You know what he's like. He wouldn't abandon Jessica when she needs him most."

Elizabeth bit her lip. "He's abandoned me," she choked out. "He doesn't think I need a sympathetic friend."

Enid looked over, close to tears herself. "You have been pretty difficult to approach, you know," she said with concern. "Maybe they're trying to figure out a way of helping you. Maybe it's you they're talking about."

Elizabeth turned her face back to the street. "I can imagine what they're saying about me," she said.

Imagining that the tennis ball was the jaw of Jake Jacoby, Bruce whacked it over the net with all the force he had.

His opponent, a new member of the country

club, lost his balance trying to reach it, and fell at the side of the court.

"Give me a break, will you, Bruce?" he called. "I told you I haven't been playing that long."

Bruce tipped his racket. "Sorry," he said. "I'm really sorry."

He moved back from the net. The thing he was really sorry about was that he hadn't decked that creep Jacoby when he had the chance. *Just once,* Bruce thought as he got ready to serve again. *That's all I want. To hit him just once.* Maybe then he'd be able to stop thinking about Friday night. Bruce tossed the ball in the air, imagining the exact point on Jake Jacoby's chin that he would land his punch. Maybe then he'd be able to stop thinking about Pamela.

Wham!

"What are you trying to do, kill me?"

Bruce's attention came back to the court. His opponent was sprawled on the ground again, this time wincing in pain as he rubbed his ankle.

"I'm sorry," Bruce apologized again. "I really am."

The other boy slowly got to his feet. "I've had enough," he said, shaking his head. "If I wanted to be wounded in active combat, I'd join the Marines, not play tennis."

Bruce watched him as the boy limped back

toward the clubhouse. His mind was back at the Box Tree. Why had he acted like such a coward? Whether Pamela was worth fighting over or not, he had his own pride to think of. Not letting creeps like that think he was afraid of them was worth a bloody nose.

Pamela's image came into Bruce's mind as he slowly followed the other boy from the court. There was a stubborn, stupid, irrational part of him that thought she was worth fighting for, too. No matter how hard he argued with it, it refused to budge. He kept seeing the look on her face when the Big Mesa troublemakers had come up to them the other night. Even though he didn't remember noticing the pain in her eyes then, he saw it clearly now. She'd looked as though someone were stepping on her heart. Bruce sliced the air with his racket as he climbed the slope leading to the locker room. For that alone he should have hit Jacoby.

The locker room was warm and humid, and smelled of sweaty socks and men's colognes. It was filled with guys laughing and talking about gas mileage and guitar riffs and what team was a certain for the pennant next year.

Bruce sighed with relief as he crossed the room. This was the one place he felt safe from Pamela. She didn't follow him in here, staring at him with her hypnotic blue eyes, pleading with him to understand. It was too bad he couldn't stay in here until he got over her and the mess she'd made of his heart.

Bruce jerked open his locker. His own reflection gazed back at him from the mirror on the door. *How long will it take?* he wondered. He could stay out of Big Mesa indefinitely, that would help. And he could spend a lot of time here, changing in and out of his tennis clothes. But how long would it take for him to get over Pamela once and for all? Six months? A year? Two years? Three?

Bruce slammed the door shut again. At least she didn't go to school in Sweet Valley. Then the answer to his question might be "forever."

"You're bound to be lucky this time," Olivia was saying.

Nicholas frowned at the phone. "Isn't that what they told Napoleon on the eve of the Battle of Waterloo?" he asked.

"You know what they say," said Olivia breezily. "Third time's the charm."

"Three strikes and you're out is what they say," grumbled Nicholas. "I'll probably be lucky to come back from this date alive."

Olivia's laughter—a sound that used to fill him with a warm, happy feeling—cackled over the line. "Cheer up, Nick," she ordered. "At least it'll all be over after tonight."

"It'll all be over because I'll be a wreck," he shot back. "I'll tell you one thing, Olivia. I'm swearing off women forever after this. I've really learned my lesson this time. Some guys are lucky in love, and some guys just aren't. It's like either having a talent for cooking or not being able to boil water."

"And you're saying you can't boil water?"

He could picture the ironic smile on her face. "Yes, Olivia, that's what I'm saying. I don't even know how to turn on the stove."

Olivia sighed. "You think this whole thing was a big mistake, don't you? You're blaming me."

Even though she couldn't see him, Nicholas shook his head. "I'm not blaming you. Everyone knows you artistic types have too much imagination. I'm blaming myself. I'm the one who should have known better."

"Oh, come on," Olivia coaxed. "Hasn't this *Hunks* thing been at least a little bit better than sitting at home on the weekend all by yourself?"

"Only if your home happens to be located in the center of a black hole," said Nicholas.

At least you've finally figured out how to play it, Nicholas congratulated himself as he jumped into the jeep Sunday night for his third

Hunks date. *Easy come, easy go. No stress, no mess.*

On the first two dates he'd spent time worrying about what he would wear. He'd been ready long before he needed to be. He'd spent hours thinking about where they should go. And what had happened? He was always dressed wrong, his date was always late, and they never went where he wanted to go.

So this time he hadn't given any thought to the evening at all. He was wearing the same shirt and pants he'd been wearing all day to work in the garden; he hadn't even looked up the address on the city map yet; and he hadn't given one second's thought to where they might go.

Whistling a carefree tune, Nicholas fastened his seat belt and reached for the map. "Paloma Drive," he muttered to himself, his finger moving down the page. There was no Paloma Drive in the street list. "There has to be," he informed the empty car. "There just has to be. She told me there was." He ran through the Ps again. There wasn't.

Nicholas turned on the ignition. "Well, she said it's near Shelter Cove," he reminded himself. "I'll just head there."

By the time Nicholas finally found Ann Hunter's house, the jeep looked as though he'd driven across the country in it. There were more dead ends and unpaved roads in Southern California than he'd ever imagined, and most of them seemed to be around Shelter Cove. By the end he knew Shelter Cove so well he could have drawn a map of it, and unlike any other map of the area, it would also include Paloma Drive.

Ann answered the door so quickly he knew she must have been waiting at the window.

"I was afraid you weren't coming," she said as she opened the door. "I thought maybe you got cold feet."

He couldn't speak at first, he was so surprised. Ann had looked all right the night of the *Hunks* show, but tonight she was beautiful. It wasn't just that she'd obviously gone to a lot of trouble, it was also because she wasn't nervous and embarrassed. Instead she seemed so self-possessed that she was almost serene. There was something about her—either her easy calm or the mischievous way she was smiling at him—that reminded Nicholas of an angel in a Renaissance painting.

He shuffled awkwardly, finally taking in the fact that Ann was not only beautiful, she was dressed in a stunning white sheath, as though she thought they'd be going somewhere fancy. Suddenly uncomfortably aware of the grass stains on his pants and the faint aroma of fertilizer coming from his shoes, Nicholas folded his arms across his chest, hoping she didn't notice the tomato-sauce stain on his shirt from lunch.

"It was the map," he finally managed to explain. He couldn't take his eyes off her. "It doesn't list Paloma Drive."

Ann groaned. "Oh, Nicholas, I'm really sorry. It's my fault completely."

The way she said his name made him feel as though they were already friends.

"I should've asked if you had a new map. Paloma Drive's only existed for a couple of years."

"Oh, right," he nodded his head, suddenly aware that he didn't have even a flower to give her. He grinned foolishly. "Well, I'm here now."

"Why don't you come in for a minute?" she asked, holding the door open. "I'm not quite ready."

She looked ready to him. What more could she do, put on her wings?

"Just take a seat," she told him, waving toward the living room. "I'll be right back."

But he couldn't sit down. Nicholas had gone through the day like a man half asleep, but now he was suddenly charged with energy. *No, not energy,* he told himself as he paced the bright and cheerful room. *Excitement.* For the first time in ages he was actually excited about a

181

date. *Calm down,* he warned himself. *The night's young. It could still end in tears.*

"Sorry to keep you waiting," Ann said from behind him.

He turned around. Instead of the sophisticated white dress she'd been wearing before, she was now wearing slacks and a casual top.

"You've changed!"

She gave him a wink. "I couldn't very well go out in a cocktail dress when you're dressed like that, could I?" she asked with a good-natured laugh. "People would think I was dating the gardener."

This evening may end in tears, Nicholas was thinking, *but they'll be tears of joy.*

Laughing at a joke Ann had just made, he leaned back in his chair as the waiter put the bill in front of him. He couldn't believe how right Olivia had been. Third time was the charm. Not only was Ann human, unattached, and a non-giggler, she was funny, intelligent, attractive, and great company. He wished he hadn't wasted any time with Jakki and Susan. He wished he'd had all three of his dates with Ann.

"So what do you want to do next?" he asked. "I'm open to suggestions."

Ann shook her head. "I picked the restaurant; you have to make the next choice. It's only fair."

"What about the amusement park?" he asked immediately. He could see them sitting at the top of the Ferris wheel, looking down at the lights below.

She clapped her hands. "That's perfect! I love amusement parks."

"Great." Nicholas grinned. "I'll just pay the check and we can go." He reached for his wallet, then frowned.

Ann leaned forward. "What's the matter?" she asked. "You look like you just found a scorpion in your pocket."

"I didn't find *anything* in my pocket," he answered, trying not to show the panic he was feeling. Having checked his pants, he started going through his jacket.

"Do you think you lost it?"

He shook his head, checking his pants again. "I'm not sure."

"Maybe you dropped it in the Jeep?"

His hand was in his inside jacket pocket for the third time when he saw his wallet very clearly in his mind, right where he'd left it on the top of his dresser.

"I don't believe this," he moaned. "I took it out this morning because I was afraid I might drop it on the lawn while I was working, and I never put it back." Nicholas started thinking fast. Maybe he could leave her here, go home, get his wallet . . .

Ann reached over and snatched the bill from in front of him. "That's the great advantage of being a woman," she said with a laugh. "You always keep your wallet in your purse."

Nicholas still had some hope of the evening ending in tears of joy even after they got the flat. After all, it could happen to anyone who took a shortcut and got lost in the middle of nowhere, couldn't it? Not to Ann, of course, who had told him all along he was going the wrong way. But to any other, more normal person, who didn't really have much of a sense of direction, it could easily happen.

And it could happen to anyone that they couldn't figure out how to work the jack, couldn't it? Not to Ann, of course; she seemed to have been raised with one in her back pocket, but to another, more normal person, who had only changed a tire once before in his entire life, of course it could happen.

Nicholas watched from his front porch as Ann got into the cab he'd called to take her home. No, it wasn't until he had thrown up on the roller coaster that he realized exactly what sort of tears were going to end the evening. And who would be crying them.

It was the first time all night she'd been wrong about anything. He'd told her that he didn't like roller coasters because of a bad experience when he was seven. He'd warned her. But she'd been so excited to go on it that in the end he'd let her enthusiasm persuade him. *It's all just a question of mind over matter,* he'd told himself as the attendant locked them in. *Mind over matter, that's all it is.* But it wasn't. It was a question of matter all over the car. And then, to add to his humiliation, he was so sick, Ann had had to drive him home.

Nicholas slowly climbed the stairs to his room with a sinking heart. Tomorrow he would be back on *Hunks*, and the entire nation would know what sort of a date he'd been. If he weren't feeling so ill, he might leave the country while he still had the chance.

Steven was exhausted by the time he got back to his apartment. He couldn't tell anymore which of his sisters he was more worried about. He didn't envy Elizabeth what she'd already gone through, or the ordeal ahead of her, but at least she had more than a fighting chance. Anyone who knew her knew that there was no way the accident could have been caused by any negligent behavior on her part. And now that he was sure there had been another car, they at least knew what to look for. But Jessica was something else.

185

Throwing his bag over his shoulder, Steven slowly climbed the steps to his building. It was impossible to tell what was going on in Jessica's mind. It seemed obvious to him that the shock of Sam's death had had an enormous impact on her, but he couldn't help thinking that there was something else wrong. Why should Jessica be so angry with Elizabeth? Elizabeth had always been closer to her than anyone else. And, after all, the accident might have killed her, too.

Steven was so preoccupied with his own thoughts that his key was already in the lock when he noticed a note taped to the door. He pulled it off and leaned against the door frame.

Dear Steven Wakefield, it said. I came by as we'd agreed, but you weren't here. I hope you don't mind, but the landlord was around and he offered to show me the apartment. It looks great. Ideal. So if you have no objections, I'll arrange to move in Monday afternoon. I can understand, though, if you want to meet me first. I've got classes from eight A.M. *on tomorrow, but if you get home early enough tonight, give me a call and I'll come over. I'm really looking forward to meeting you. Quite a few of my friends seem to know you, and they all think you're great.*

It was signed *Billie Winkler.*

Steven dropped the note on the hall table as he entered the apartment. Well, Billie Winkler was going to have to wait until tomorrow to meet him. Steven was too tired to see him tonight, and besides, he needed the room rented as quickly as possible. Unless Billie Winkler turned out to be a heavy-metal drummer with insomnia, he was going to have to do.

Boy, do I hope I like him, Steven thought as he locked the door and went straight to his room. The last thing he needed was another problem in his life.

It was the bus's fault. The bus was cramped and noisy and it smelled like a toilet. It smelled just like the toilet Margo had been locked in once when she was very little. It had been dark and smelly, and she cried and cried, but no one let her out. That was why it was the bus's fault that she was beginning to feel so confused. Every time they stopped somewhere, she thought they'd already stopped there before. She couldn't tell if they were going west or east. She was sure people were shiftily glancing up from their papers to look at her. And she was hungry. She was so hungry. . . . And the voice had gone silent. It was because of the bus; Margo knew that. It was because the bus was so noisy and it smelled so bad, but the voice had stopped. If Margo were a weakling she would have started crying, but she wasn't weak, she was very, very strong. Her knuckles were white as she gripped her bag. *I'm very, very strong,* she told herself over and over. *Very, very strong.*

And then, in Houston, Margo decided to leave the bus because of a song playing outside. It was called "Money." Margo's feet started tapping as soon as she heard it. *That's what I need,* thought Margo. *Money.* She had miscalculated, somehow. She had enough only for one more can of soda and maybe three more candy bars. But Albuquerque was farther away than a soda and three candy bars. *Money . . . a lot of money . . .*

And then she realized that it was a sign. The song was a sign, a sign that she should get off here. The voice was too tired to talk to her directly, but this was its way of guiding her. This was its way of telling her to get off the bus, and then she'd have money. She'd have all the money she needed. She'd know exactly what to do.

"Wait!" she screamed as the driver started to shut the doors. "Wait! I have to get out!"

It was so hot outside that she nearly keeled over. And the song had changed. Instead of "Money," it was "Town Without Pity."

Chapter 9

It was a typical Monday morning on Calico
Drive. Alice Wakefield was standing at the back
door calling Prince Albert in from the yard for
his breakfast. Ned Wakefield was thundering
down the stairs, muttering about being late for
work. Jessica sang along with the radio in her
room as she got ready for school. Everyone's life
was continuing as it always had. They were all
carrying on, moving forward.

Everyone but Elizabeth.

Get up! Elizabeth told herself as she lay in
bed listening to her family prepare for the day.
Get up, get dressed, make some plans!

She closed her eyes, trying to get back the
feeling she had had yesterday before she saw

the Jeep parked outside of Todd's house: the feeling that she was almost human again; that things were going to be OK, even for her.

Get up, Elizabeth told herself more sternly. *Forget about the Jeep. Forget about Todd and Jessica. It doesn't mean anything. Enid's right; she needs a friend, that's all. He's just helping her out.*

Jessica's bedroom door banged shut and Elizabeth could hear her twin racing down the stairs.

Elizabeth thought about Steven. Steven had helped her remember about the lights. Steven was sure there'd been another car. Steven and her father were going to prove her innocence. Everything was going to be all right. They had promised her.

Elizabeth took a deep breath and forced herself out of bed. Until things did go back to the way they'd been, she'd just have to pretend that they were.

Elizabeth took one of her favorite outfits out of the closet and began to get dressed. She wasn't going back to school, but she could still do something. She could do the homework Enid had brought over and she could take Prince Albert for a walk later.

As she washed up, she decided that maybe this afternoon she might even try to write a poem.

Standing in the hallway outside the kitchen for a few seconds, Elizabeth listened to her mother and sister talking while they finished breakfast. It might have been any morning of any year. Mrs. Wakefield was worried that it might rain, and Jessica was worried about a split end.

If you act like everything's OK, it'll be OK, she assured herself. *You have to try.* Taking a deep breath, she pushed open the kitchen door. "Good morning," she said as brightly as she could manage.

Mrs. Wakefield looked up with a smile. "Well, look at you!" she exclaimed, obviously pleased to see Elizabeth up and dressed and out of her room. "Don't you look nice today."

The smile left Jessica's face as though a switch had been thrown. She took a last swallow of juice and got to her feet.

"Jessica," said Mrs. Wakefield. "Aren't you going to say good morning to your sister?"

In answer, Jessica turned her back on the room, scooping up her books from the counter. "I'll be home late," she said, as though her mother hadn't spoken. "Todd's taking me to watch the *Hunks* taping this afternoon. We'll probably go for pizza or something afterward."

The screen door slammed.

"Aren't you going too?" Mrs. Wakefield

asked, turning to look at Elizabeth.

But Elizabeth wasn't there. Elizabeth was running back up the stairs.

"Hey, Bruce!"

Bruce shut his locker and turned around. Todd Wilkins, Scott Trost, and Artie Western were coming down the hall behind him. "What's up?" he asked.

"You coming to the *Hunks* taping?" Todd asked.

Artie grinned. "A bunch of us thought we'd go and give Nick our moral support," he said. "I was talking to Olivia at lunch, and she said Nick was still in a state of shock, he had such a bad weekend."

Well, he wasn't the only one, Bruce thought.

Scott laughed, shaking his head. "Can you imagine? Three dates with three different girls in three days, and each one was worse than the next." He rolled his eyes. "Apparently Nick says that if there were a prize for Dating Disaster of the Decade, it would be a three-way tie."

I'll bet I could break the tie, Bruce thought. *Next time I'll send him out with Pamela and the Big Mesa Bozos.*

"Poor Nick," said Todd. "He sure doesn't have much luck with women."

"Who does?" asked Bruce. He'd meant it as a

joke, but somehow it didn't come out quite the way he'd intended.

Todd looked uncomfortable. "They are . . . um . . . they can be difficult, can't they?" he asked.

Scott nodded. "It's true," he said. "They always make things difficult. You think everything's going to be fine, and then a girl comes along and suddenly everything's messed up."

Or impossible, thought Bruce.

"Olivia says Nick's first date not only made him go to Club Mud, she wanted him to stay for the amateur wrestling match," put in Artie. He looked from one boy to the next. "Can you imagine Nick *wrestling*?"

"I don't think I've ever seen that show," said Bruce. He swung his book bag over his shoulder. "What's going to happen this afternoon? Does Nick get to tell how awful his dates were?"

Artie shook his head. "You wish. His dates get to tell the entire country how awful *Nick* was."

Scott pretended to shudder. "Geez, it could turn you off dating forever. No wonder guys become monks."

Todd looked at Bruce. "So what do you say? You going to come along and give Nick some support?"

Bruce shrugged. "I don't know. I've really got

a lot on my mind at the moment. . . ."

Artie gave him a shove. "Oh, come on, Patman. It'll be fun."

Just behind Artie's head, Bruce saw a dark, slender girl disappear into the principal's office. His heart slammed against his rib cage. It was Pamela. He was sure it was. What was she doing *here?*

"Yeah, come on, Bruce," said Scott. "We'll have some laughs."

Bruce wondered how much fun the other diners at the Box Tree had had the other night, watching him being taunted by the Big Mesa boys. He wondered how many laughs they'd had at his expense when they got home.

"Count me out," Bruce snapped. "I can't think of anything less funny than watching poor Nick being humiliated on network television by a bunch of girls." He turned around, suddenly in a hurry. He didn't want to be standing here when Pamela left.

"What's wrong with you, Patman?" Artie shouted after him. "Was it something we said?"

Jessica entered the *Hunks* studio that afternoon by herself, scanning the packed studio for a familiar face. It wasn't true, what she'd told her mother, that Todd was taking her to the taping. In fact, the only reason she'd decided to go herself was because he'd mentioned that he and some of the guys were planning to go.

There he was, over on the side, sitting between Artie Western and Scott Trost.

"Jessica! Jessica, we're over here!"

Jessica recognized Amy's voice. Amy must have come with Caroline and Lila. She didn't turn around. Instead, Jessica started walking toward where Todd was sitting, a bewildered, lost expression on her face.

"Jessica!"

This time, when she heard Scott calling her, she looked over immediately.

"Hey, Jessica," said Scott. "Are you all alone? Why don't you sit with us?"

Jessica's eyes moved from Scott to Artie to Todd. "Oh, I don't want to intrude—"

"What are you talking about?" Artie stood up to let her pass. "You're not intruding, is she, Todd?"

Todd smiled warmly at her. "Of course not," he said, moving over so she could have his seat. "How could you even think a thing like that?"

"So what are you saying, Jakki?" asked Buddy, grinning emcee of *Hunks*. He winked at the audience. "Are you saying that Nicholas here didn't turn out to be the date of your dreams?"

195

Jakki snorted.

That's what that sound was, Nicholas said to himself, trying to wish himself invisible. *It wasn't a laugh. It wasn't a giggle, thank God. It was a pure animal snort.*

"Are you kidding?" Jakki demanded. Today, in honor of the occasion, even her fingernails were black. "He was the drag of my dreams, that's what he was. I'd have more fun with guys who were asleep."

Laughing and giggling was what the audience was doing.

"You surprise me," Buddy said with a leer at camera three. He put a hand on Nicholas's shoulder. "I'd have said that Nick looks like a young man who knows how to show a girl a good time, but you seem to think differently."

Jakki rolled her eyes and snorted again. The effect was strangely horselike. "He wouldn't know how to show a girl a good time if it came in a box," said Jakki. She leaned directly into camera one. "Can you believe it?" she asked the audience. "We weren't in the club more than two minutes, and he was ready to go home."

Buddy floated over to Susan, who had managed to find a dress to wear this evening.

"And what about you, Susan?" Buddy asked. He raised his eyebrows at the audience. "You're obviously a very different type of girl from Jakki here. Would you say that Nicholas was the date of your dreams?"

Susan opened her mouth, presumably to speak, but all that came out was a burst of laughter.

Buddy grinned at the front row. "Doesn't sound like Prince Charming, does it?" he asked. He turned back to Susan. "Come on, Susie," he said coaxingly. "You can't just laugh hysterically. You have to tell us what you thought. Was Nicholas really that bad?"

Nicholas thought longingly of the old amateur shows where a trapdoor would suddenly open and swallow you up. He wasn't sure which of them he wanted swallowed, though—him or Susan.

Susan was laughing so hard now that she could hardly stay in her seat. She nodded her head.

Buddy squatted near her chair, holding the microphone up. It sounded like a flock of geese were passing.

"Was he boring?" Buddy prompted. "What did he do wrong?"

The audience watched as Susan struggled to gain control of herself. When the giggles had finally subsided, she gripped her chair with both hands and looked into camera two. She took a deep breath.

"Well?" asked Buddy. "People want to know."

"Everything," Susan managed to gasp before a fresh wave of laughter took her over once more.

The entire studio was in hysterics. Nicholas smiled bravely into the sea of faces, thankful that the bright lights kept him from identifying anyone. His friends had come to give him moral support, but he recognized more than one laugh out there as belonging to someone he knew. He was never going to live this down. Not if he lived to be a thousand.

Buddy moved over to Ann, and Nicholas's eyes moved over to Ann too. This was it. This was the big one. If there were one person left in the universe who wasn't laughing at him, that person would be in hysterics by the time she got through describing their date. Nicholas glanced desperately toward the exit. Maybe he should just make a bolt for it now, while he still had the chance.

"And now we come to our last contestant, the lovely Ann," Buddy was saying. "Ann, Jakki and Susan here have described Nicholas as the boy you wouldn't go out with on a bet. What do you say? Is he as bad as they think?"

Nicholas held his breath, Ann's voice filling up his mind. *He turned up looking and smelling like the gardener, and then he got lost and didn't know how to change the tire on his own car, and then he didn't have any money to pay for dinner, and then he threw up all over me on the roller coaster.*

It took a few minutes for him to realize that something was wrong. The audience wasn't laughing. The stagehands weren't doubled over in the wings. Buddy was nodding solemnly, his smile sweet and sincere. Even Susan wasn't spluttering away.

Nicholas looked over at Ann.

"It was so romantic," she was saying. "We went to a fabulous restaurant right on the beach, and then we went to an amusement park. If you can imagine what it's like sitting up among the stars with a handsome boy who not only knows all the constellations, but can tell you the myths behind each one . . ." She smiled at Buddy and camera one. "It was just incredible. I felt like a princess."

Nicholas's eyes met hers. She had a radiant smile.

Buddy took Ann's hand and pulled her to her feet, leading her across the stage.

"Well, what do you know . . ." Buddy said, grinning at the audience. "Nicholas," he said, nodding. "Nicholas, come over here." He grabbed Nicholas with his free hand. "It looks like you and Ann really hit it off."

The audience whistled and clapped.

Nicholas, weak with relief, could only wish he'd known he and Ann had hit it off. It would have saved him at least one sleepless night. He glanced over at Ann. She was still smiling at him.

Buddy put an arm around each of them. "What do you say?" he asked. "Would you like to go on another date, the two of you?"

Nicholas couldn't speak. What if she'd only said all that stuff to be kind? What if she'd rather go on a date with Buddy than with him?

And then Buddy stepped away and Nicholas was standing beside Ann, looking into her eyes.

"Only if you let me do the planning this time, OK?" she whispered.

Even though he'd never kissed a girl on television before, it was the only response he could think of.

The audience went wild.

How did we wind up here? Todd wondered. The guys had all wanted to stop at a burrito stand after the show, but Jessica had refused to join them. Sam had loved burritos, she'd whispered to Todd; she couldn't possibly go with them. And then she'd looked at him with all the sadness and loneliness in the world in those big blue eyes, and he'd known he couldn't go either.

He'd feel like a complete creep, eating bean burritos while Jessica rode home all by herself, crying over Sam. "Maybe you could give me a lift home," he'd said. "It's a long drive for you on your own."

And now here they were, walking along the same beach that they'd walked along the other night.

"You should have gone with the other guys," Jessica said in a low, flat voice. "I feel like I'm ruining all your fun."

The evening was chilly, and she'd put on a sweater that had been in the back of the Jeep, a sweater he'd seen Elizabeth wear at least a hundred times. It confused him so much that he had to jam his hands in his pockets to keep from reaching out for her.

"Don't be silly," he said, trying to make his eyes stay on the sand. "I can have a burrito any time. I'd much rather be here with you."

"Really?" She looked over at him.

It was amazing how sometimes she looked more like Elizabeth than Elizabeth herself. And it wasn't because they were identical; it was something else. Some expression in her eyes.

Todd nodded, taking a step to the left as she took a step to the left. "Yeah, really."

Jessica stopped, tracing half a heart in the sand with her toe. "It's just that the show made me feel so . . . so lonely." She rubbed the drawing out almost as soon as it was done. "I know it's silly, it's only a show . . . but . . ."

"It's not silly," Todd whispered. "I know what you mean." He did know. For some reason, the show had made him feel lonely too. Todd had seen the look Ann and Nicholas exchanged right before they kissed, and he'd felt as though his heart would break. There was something between them—something personal and secret and real. Something that only they would ever know about. He remembered looking at Elizabeth like that, and he wanted to cry.

This time when Jessica moved closer he didn't move farther away.

The light was fading and the sea was misty. When she stepped into his arms he could almost believe it was Elizabeth. When she put her arms around him, he felt Elizabeth's touch. It was her heart he heard beating, her breath on his cheek.

But it was Jessica's lips that met his own.

Lila parked the Triumph in the garage after school, surprised to see her father's car in the driveway. She glanced at her watch. It was much too early for him to be home. The moon wasn't out yet. He must have gotten to the office some other way today.

Lila grabbed her books out of the backseat

and strolled into the house, grateful that it was the maid's night off and she wouldn't have to talk to anyone. Between school and the *Hunks* taping, it had been a long day, and she was looking forward to a nice hot bath and dinner in front of the television. Sometimes being alone wasn't such a bad thing.

Her foot was on the first step of the staircase to the second floor when she heard voices coming from the living room. She could recognize her father's deep bass, but the other voice was low and muffled and hard to distinguish. Lila stopped, looking toward the large carved door.

That's funny, she thought. She frowned, genuinely puzzled. Not only did Mr. Fowler rarely get home before dark, but it wasn't like him to bring guests back without warning her first. She stepped back to the door of the living room. Should she knock? Should she just go in?

Don't be silly, Lila told herself. *If he was having a business meeting, he'd have told you so you wouldn't interrupt. Just go in. It's your home too, isn't it?*

Lila put her hand on the knob, then froze. All of a sudden she recognized the other voice. It belonged to Grace.

Lila leaned her head closer to the door. The reason she hadn't recognized her mother's voice immediately was because the only other times she'd heard it, it had been strong and confident and beautifully controlled. Now it sounded as though it were drowning.

"It's all right, Grace," Lila's father was saying. "It's all right. You're making too much out of nothing."

Lila pressed her ear against the door, hoping to catch her mother's reply, but whatever it was was lost in tears and probably her father's chest.

"I'm going to get you a strong cup of coffee," Mr. Fowler announced suddenly. "You wait here."

Not wanting to risk being caught running up the stairs, Lila ducked behind the hall table. She held her breath as her father came out of the living room, but he walked right by her. As soon as he disappeared into the kitchen, she got to her feet as silently as she could. Unable to resist, Lila peeked into the living room before she made her break for the stairs.

Grace was slumped on the sofa, her face buried in her hands, her body shaking with sobs.

Lila felt such a stab of sympathy for her mother that she almost went rushing over to throw her arms around her. It hadn't occurred to her before that she wasn't the only one who might be in pain.

Steven checked his watch as he raced across campus. He'd passed up a chance to have coffee with the prettiest girl in his sociology class because he wanted to be back at the apartment in time for his new roommate's arrival. It seemed only polite.

And anyway, Steven thought as he raced across the quad, *if he turns out to be some guy with a shaved head and a lizard tattooed on his neck, I'll be able to tell him to leave before he unpacks.* He grinned to himself as he left the campus. *OK,* he amended. *I'll be able to ask him to leave before he unpacks. And then I'll be able to offer him a cup of coffee when he says no.*

There was a beat-up gray van outside of his building. At its back, staggering slightly under the weight of an old black trunk painted with stars, was an incredibly large young man wearing a ponytail and a baseball cap.

It's all right, Steven told himself. *He's fine. I'm sure he's fine. So what if he looks like a sumo wrestler? I'm sure he has a great personality.*

"Billie?" called Steven. "Billie Winkler? I'm Steven Wakefield."

But the wrestler was shaking his head. "Uh-uh," he grunted. "I'm Pete. Billie's upstairs."

Ashamed to be feeling a little relieved, Steven nodded and continued inside.

A cowboy was coming down the stairs. He

was wearing jeans, a white shirt with silver tips on the collar, and a string tie. He was wearing a black cowboy hat with a silver and turquoise band around it. The only thing missing was his horse and a gun. But noticing the scar running down one side of the cowboy's face, Steven wasn't so sure about the gun. Steven blinked. They didn't have any cowboys in his building. He would have noticed.

The cowboy nodded at him.

Steven forced himself to speak. "Billie?" he asked. "Billie Winkler?"

The cowboy grinned. "I'm Storm," he said. "Billie's upstairs."

"Right." Steven didn't bother feeling guilty about his relief this time; he was too busy taking the stairs two at a time.

"What have I done?" he whispered under his breath. If those were Billie Winkler's friends, there was no telling what Billie himself would be like.

Steven fairly flew into the apartment. There was a young woman standing in the living room, holding a lamp. She turned around.

Well, at least his girlfriend's beautiful, Steven thought immediately. *How bad can he be with a girl like this?*

"Hi," said the girl. "You must be Steven."

It wasn't easy to speak when someone that

exquisite was smiling at him with such blindingly white teeth.

"Yeah," he managed to say. "I'm Steven."

She extended the hand that wasn't holding the lamp. "Hi. I'm Billie."

Just be patient, said the voice. *I wouldn't lead you astray. I'm looking out for you. . . .*

Margo huddled into her thin coat. She'd been sitting on this bench in the Houston train station on and off for nearly sixteen hours because the voice had told her to come here. *Never mind the buses,* the voice had said, *the bus is too slow.*

Margo watched a small boy cross the station with a hot dog in his hands. Margo's stomach was so empty that she wasn't really hungry anymore, but at the sight of the hot dog she had such a desire to jump up and snatch it out of the little kid's hands that she stopped herself just in time. It wouldn't do to bring attention to herself. Not now. It would make the voice angry.

Margo's eyes scanned the waiting room again. She was waiting for another sign. It hadn't come yet, but Margo could be patient. She was good at waiting. She'd been waiting her whole life. Waiting to go home.

There was a crackle, and then the loudspeaker blared across the room. "The five forty-five from Los Angeles has just arrived on track two. Passengers wishing to connect here for other destinations should consult the board in the main lobby."

The only words Margo heard were "Los Angeles." L.A. Her home.

Her gray eyes narrowed as a stream of people came out of gate two.

You see, Margo? the voice purred. *I was looking after you. Look what I'm sending you now.*

Margo looked. Waddling under the weight of several bags was a small, elderly woman with a cherry-red straw hat on her head and a white chiffon scarf around her neck.

What good was an old woman going to do her? Old women just smelled bad and yelled at you all the time. Old women made you do all the hard jobs, and made you watch them eat while you were hungry. They gave their cats better food than they gave you. Old women. Margo didn't like old women. Old women smelled.

This old women nodded as she sat down, then she put her things on the bench between them.

Margo didn't return the nod. She was staring at the newspaper sticking out of one of the shopping bags. Margo's heart began to gallop.

What was the voice doing to her? Had she been tricked? Was this some kind of game, some kind of joke?

Margo couldn't breathe. Her heart was beating so hard she could barely breathe. Because the voice was playing a horrible joke on her. The old woman had a picture of Margo. A picture of Margo on the front of her newspaper. Margo was smiling.

Wild with terror, Margo made a lunge for the paper.

"Oh, I'm afraid you can't have that," said the old woman, snatching it back so fast Margo couldn't stop her. "It's for my daughter. I promised I'd bring her a copy of our hometown paper." She smiled, showing her teeth. "You know what a treat that sort of thing is."

"Oh, yes," said Margo. "I know."

The old woman asked if Margo would watch her things while she went to the restroom. "You have no idea what it's like to be old," she told Margo.

Margo said, "Of course."

"You can look at my paper while I'm gone," said the old woman.

"Thank you," said Margo. She took the paper in her hands.

Trust me, Margo, said the voice. *Look at*

that picture. Do you have blond hair? Do you live in California? Have you been indicted for involuntary manslaughter?

It wasn't Margo. The voice was right. It was a photograph of another girl, a girl so used to smiling that she had a dimple in her left cheek. A girl who lived in California. In Sweet Valley, California.

Sweet Valley. That sounded like just the sort of place Margo's family would live. Sweet Valley. It was just the sort of place she belonged.

But Margo needed money to get to Sweet Valley. She needed food. She needed to sleep somewhere other than on this hard bench.

Most people buy round-trip tickets, the voice was saying. *Most old women who visit their daughters bring plenty of cash.*

Margo put the paper on top of the old woman's bags and walked slowly toward the rest room, thinking about the scarf around the old lady's neck. Thinking about the cherry-red hat. Thinking about the white straw purse she had clutched under her arm.

"If my daughter comes, tell her I won't be long," the old lady had told her. "Tell her I'll be right out."

Margo smiled as she opened the restroom door.

Poor old lady. You're going to be longer than

you thought. Margo's feet echoed across the tiles. She stooped down to look under the stalls. There was only one pair of feet. Old lady's feet. *Much, much longer,* Margo said to herself as the door swung open and she slammed the old woman back against the wall. *Much, much longer than you thought.*

Get ready for Jessica and Elizabeth's hottest adventures ever when they go to **SWEET VALLEY UNIVERSITY** *!*

Join Lila, Todd, Enid, and all your favorite Sweet Valley characters as they become wilder and *wiser in* College Girls, *due in October!*

Here's an exciting excerpt from
SVU #1, College Girls

In the clear autumn afternoon, the campus of Sweet Valley University looked even prettier and more perfect than it had in the colorful brochures. From the sun-dappled, tree-lined streets, to the beautiful red-tiled buildings, to the groups of students laughing and talking as they strolled across the lawns, everything about the campus seemed to say, "Welcome to college. Welcome to freedom."

"We made it!" Jessica shouted as she followed Todd's BMW through the univeristy gates. She sounded the horn. "Hello, freedom, here I come!"

Elizabeth couldn't surpress an unexpected ripple of excitement herself. Her sister was right; they had made it! They really had! They weren't little kids anymore. They weren't just visiting their brother, Steven. This was where they lived now. She was a college freshman, an adult in the real world.

"I love it, I love it, I love it," Jessica squealed. "I really do." She gestured out the window. "Look at it, Liz!" she ordered. "Isn't it beautiful?"

Elizabeth looked. Although it was the beginning of freshman orientation and classes wouldn't begin for another week, it looked as though the entire student body had already arrived for a week of fun. And Jessica was right, it was beautiful.

Elizabeth smiled happily as she gazed out the window. She could see herself walking down the steps of the library. She could see herself sitting on one of the wooden benches along the pathways, reading a book. She could imagine herself throwing a Frisbee on the lawn with Todd.

College was going to be great.

As she walked toward the campus coffee bar, Jessica couldn't help thinking how lucky she was. She'd been at Sweet Valley University for only a few fantastic hours, and already she'd made friends with Isabella Ricci, one of the most popular and fabulous sophomores on campus. Jessica couldn't help smiling to herself as she strutted across the lawn. She'd been missing her best friend, Lila Fowler, a lot the last few days. Not just because she was concerned about Lila's whereabouts, but because Elizabeth had Todd and Enid to talk to, but she didn't really have anyone to share her own excitement with. Now Jessica had Isabella Ricci. Isabella was even more beautiful and sophisticated than Lila. And she knew *everybody* who was anybody, and had dated almost every eligible man on campus.

Jessica caught sight of the clock tower at the end of the quad and started to hurry. It was almost six thirty. She'd promised Isabella she'd meet her at six thirty because there was a jazz trio playing in the cafe this evening.

She was running as she came up the path that ran behind the cafe, but as soon she turned the corner she slowed down. When she walked through the doors of the cafe it was with the step of a woman who had seen it all. She stopped just inside the entrance. She kept her expression slightly bored, but inside she was bubbling with enthusiasm. Dark and cramped, with posters and paintings hanging on its brick walls, the cafe looked like something out of a French movie. The students sitting at the candlelit wooden tables, all of them nearly as sophisticated as Isabella, were talking in low, intimate voices, and drinking coffee from small white cups. *You can have your gondola, Lila,* Jessica thought to herself. *I'd much rather be here.*

As casually as she could, she looked around the room. Thank God, the trio hadn't even set up yet. She would have died of mortification if she'd had to walk through them while they were playing.

Jessica shook her head, and her golden hair shimmered in the subdued light. Jessica didn't have to look to know that she was creating a sensation. She'd spent the whole afternoon working on making an entrance, imitating the way she'd seen Isabella walk and stand and gaze around a room, and so far it hadn't let her down. She could feel the eyes sizing her up; the girls with envy, the guys with admiration.

At a table in the corner, she saw the long white neck and touseled black hair of Isabella Ricci against the red wall of the coffee bar. She looked as though she must be thinking of something incredibly romantic. In high school, Jessica would have waved, but not now. Now she was a college woman, not a little girl. She raised her head ever so slightly, just enough to let Isabella know that she'd seen her, and then she crossed the coffee bar like a model walking down a catwalk; like Isabella Ricci crossing a street.

Jessica had heard of people who went

216

through their entire lives without ever under-standing why they'd been born. There always seemed to be people in TV dramas and the kind of books they made you read in English who had no idea what their lives were about. They spent hours, or at least hundreds of pages, trudging around being miserable and sighing and won-dering why their lives had no meaning. But not Jessica. She might be only eighteen, but she knew exactly why she'd been put on this earth.

So she could go to college.

Outside room twenty-eight, Dickenson Hall was full of talk and music. Inside room twenty-eight, the only audible sound was the ticking of Elizabeth's watch.

Elizabeth, sitting on her bed with her hands folded on her lap, glanced at herself in the mir-ror on the back of the closet door. She knew that anyone who happened to see her sitting there would assume that she was about to go out to have a good time. Her hair was in a loose French braid, she was wearing her favorite cran-berry-red linen dress, and her bag and her jacket were on the bed beside her. She sighed. Yes, they'd assume that she had a heavy date or was waiting for a bunch of friends to pick her up. Elizabeth scowled at her reflection.

"Well, they'd be wrong," she said out loud.

"I'm not going anywhere. I'm all dressed up with nowhere to go."

For at least the twentieth time in the last forty minutes, her eyes turned to the intercom on the wall by the door. She couldn't bear to look at her watch again.

Laughter echoed like gunshots down the hallway. As far as she could tell, everyone who wasn't out at some special event on campus or in town was having a party in the dorm.

Probably everyone in the world but me is either out having a good time or throwing a party, she thought bitterly. *A party I'm not invited to.* Holding her breath, she dared a quick look at her watch. It was nine. Nine! That meant that she'd been sitting here, waiting for nothing, for two whole hours. Elizabeth picked up the book she'd been trying unsuccessfully to read and threw it across the room.

She'd thought that after their coffee together she and Enid would probably do something together. There was a free film showing in the moviehouse on campus, and she'd seen a poster for live jazz at the coffee bar, but Enid had other plans. "Gee, I'm sorry, Liz," she'd said. "I just assumed you and Jessica and Todd would be seeing Steven tonight, so I told some of the girls on my floor that I'd go for pizza with them."

But Jessica had never come back to the room,

218

and Todd had disappeared too. When Elizabeth had returned to the dorm and couldn't reach him on the phone, she'd been sure he must be on his way to pick her up. She'd been so sure, in fact, that she'd gotten dressed and gone to wait in the lobby for him. She'd waited until she got tired of people looking at her as though she were in the wrong place, and then she'd come back to her room.One of the girls on her hall had asked her if she wanted to go to the campus pub with her and some of her friends, and a couple of other girls had invited her to the common room to watch a movie, but Elizabeth still thought Todd would show up, and she didn't want to miss him.

"Well, I shouldn't have worried," she said to the empty room as she kicked off her shoes. "I could have gone to San Francisco, and he wouldn't have noticed."

She lay back on her bed, imagining her parents back at home, reading together in the living room. "I wonder what the girls are doing right now," her mother was probably saying. Her father would laugh. "Oh, you know them," he'd say. "Wherever they are, they'll be having a good time."

Down the hallway, several people started laughing as though they'd just heard the funniest story in the world.

But in room twenty-eight, Dickenson Hall, it was just about then that the tears began to fall.

Collect all the books in the Sweet Valley High series, now over 100 titles strong!

Ask your bookseller for these Sweet Valley Supers and Magnas.

SUPER EDITIONS:
PERFECT SUMMER
SPECIAL CHRISTMAS
SPRING BREAK
MALIBU SUMMER
WINTER CARNIVAL
SPRING FEVER

SUPER THRILLERS:
DOUBLE JEOPARDY
ON THE RUN
NO PLACE TO HIDE
DEADLY SUMMER
MURDER ON THE LINE
BEWARE THE WOLFMAN

SUPER STARS:
LILA'S STORY
BRUCE'S STORY
ENID'S STORY
OLIVIA'S STORY
TODD'S STORY

MAGNA EDITIONS:
THE WAKEFIELDS OF
SWEET VALLEY
THE WAKEFIELD LEGACY:
THE UNTOLD STORY
A NIGHT TO REMEMBER

And don't miss this sensational six-part miniseries—
Sweet Valley will never be the same!

#95 THE MORNING AFTER
#96 THE ARREST
#97 THE VERDICT
#98 THE WEDDING
#99 BEWARE THE BABY-SITTER
#100 THE EVIL TWIN (MAGNA)